The beady-eyed rat was on the loose in Joe's school.

"This is it, rat! You'd better give up before I have to get tough with you!" Wishbone said to his opponent.

There was no answer from the locker or from down the school hallway.

"So, silence is your game," he whispered. "Well, no one plays that game better than . . . Stealth Dog."

Wishbone crept down the hallway and headed into the school's science lab.

"I know he's around here somewhere, and he's close. He won't hear me coming, though. I'm silent as a panther. As quick as a fox. As brave as a grizzly bear. I have nerves of steel. Nothing can frighten me—not a lion, not a tiger, and certainly not a . . ."

Wishbone turned the corner of the lab table and found himself face to face with—

"—a rat! GAHHhhhhhh! Rat! Rat! Big Hairy Rat!" he yelled.

Other books in the Adventures of WISHBONE™ series:

Be a Wolf!

Salty Dog

The Prince and the Pooch

Robinhound Crusoe

Hunchdog of Notre Dame

Digging Up the Past

The Mutt in the Iron Muzzle

Muttketeer!

A Tale of Two Sitters *

Moby Dog *

The Pawloined Paper *

*coming soon

The Adventures of WISHBONE™

MUTTKETEER!

by Bill Crider
Based on the teleplay by Gail Schmeichel
Inspired by *The Three Musketeers*
by Alexandre Dumas

WISHBONE™ created by Rick Duffield

Big Red Chair Books™, *A Division of **Lyrick** Publishing*™

This book is a work of fiction. The characters, incidents, and dialogues are products of the author's imagination and are not to be construed as real. Any resemblance to actual events or persons, living or dead, is entirely coincidental.

 Big Red Chair Books™, *A Division of Lyrick Publishing*™
300 E. Bethany Drive, Allen, Texas 75002

©1997 Big Feats! Entertainment

Edited by Pam Pollack

Copy edited by Jonathon Brodman

Cover design by Lyle Miller

Interior illustrations by Don Punchatz

Cover concept by Kathryn Yingling

Wishbone photograph by Carol Kaelson

Library of Congress Catalog Card Number: 97-73288

ISBN: 1-57064-272-9

First printing: December 1997

10 9 8 7 6 5 4 3 2 1

To the children of Beth Yeshurun Day School

FROM THE BIG RED CHAIR . . .

Oh . . . hi! Wishbone here. You caught me right in the middle of some of my favorite things—books. Let me welcome you to THE ADVENTURES OF WISHBONE. In each of these books I have adventures with my friends in Oakdale and imagine myself as a character in one of the greatest stories of all time. This adventure takes place during the same time period as the first season of my television show, when Joe and his friends are twelve and in sixth grade. In *MUTTKETEER!*, I imagine I'm the young D'Artagnan from the swashbuckling tale *THE THREE MUSKETEERS*, by Alexandre Dumas. It's the exciting, epic adventure of friendship and sword-fighting heroes in France.

You're in for a real treat, so pull up a chair and a snack and enjoy *MUTTKETEER!*

Chapter One

*W*ishbone trotted toward the school building. He'd been sniffing for adventure all afternoon, and the school was where his nose had led him. He plunked himself down on the sidewalk for a brief wait.

This is the place, all right. The nose knows! Come on out, kids!

The bell rang, and Wishbone saw shoes thumping against the ground and pairs of legs scissoring rapidly as the students left the building. The shoes and legs that marched past Wishbone probably all belonged to great kids, but they weren't the ones the terrier was watching for.

Then Wishbone caught a glimpse of his best friend, Joe Talbot, the student he'd been waiting for. Joe was a brown-haired sixth-grader. He was dressed in white shorts, a blue plaid shirt, and a pair of sneakers. He carried his backpack, full of books and other important items. Joe's good friend Samantha Kepler was walking along with him. Wishbone liked Sam very much, and especially because she loved adventure and excitement, just like him.

She reminds me of me, Wishbone thought, as he

perked up at the arrival of his friends. He greeted them with joy. "Hey, Joe, good buddy, pal o' mine! Hi, Sam. Long time, no see!"

Joe and Sam knelt down, and they both patted Wishbone's head.

At that moment David Barnes came running out of the building and down the sidewalk. David wore green pants and sported a white vest over his shirt. He was another one of Joe's close friends, so, of course, he was Wishbone's friend, too.

"Hey, Joe!" David called, waving his arm. "Sam! Mr. Delgado wants to show us that new CD-ROM."

Samantha stood up. "Oh, great! I forgot about that. Come on, Joe. See you later, Wishbone."

"*Later?*" Wishbone echoed. "What's this 'later' stuff? I've been waiting for you guys all day! Okay . . . maybe not *all* day, but for hours . . . well . . . minutes, anyway."

Joe stood up beside Samantha. "You're right, Sam. I've heard that new CD is really neat. Let's go back inside and check it out."

"Well, how do you like that?" Wishbone said. "I want a look at that CD-ROM, too. I know all about CD-ROMs. Wait up, you guys! You'll probably need me to show you how it works!"

Wishbone ran toward the schoolhouse door, but he was too late to follow his friends inside. The door closed just as he reached it.

"Guys? Helllooo! Open the door, please."

But no one came to open the door, so Wishbone began to scratch at it.

"Hey, this isn't fair. I want to go to school, just like Joe, Sam, and David. I want to be one of the few . . . the proud . . . the educated!"

There was no response to Wishbone's scratching, but he still didn't give up his attempt to gain entrance into the building. "Hey, in there! Joe? Sam? David? Door, please!"

Almost as if his friends had heard him, the door popped open, and Wishbone was surprised.

"That's more like it, guys. I knew you wouldn't forget me. . . . Whoa! Wait a minute. You're not Joe."

Wishbone looked at the man who had opened the door and recognized Mr. Brassfield, the school's custodian. Wishbone barked to get Mr. Brassfield's attention. Then he sat up in a begging position.

"Hello, sir. I'm the young Jack Russell terrier, reporting for the CD-ROM demonstration."

"No dogs are allowed inside the school," Mr. Brassfield said, looking down at Wishbone.

Mr. Brassfield sprayed water from a bottle onto one of the door's window panes. Wishbone watched as he wiped it off.

"No dogs allowed in the school?" Wishbone said.

"An excellent rule. I agree with you one hundred percent. I'll be sure to tell any dogs that I happen to see. I'm here to check out the new CD-ROM, myself."

Mr. Brassfield pointed the spray bottle at Wishbone. "Go on, mutt. Get out of here."

Wishbone looked around. "Mutt? Did you say *mutt?*"

Mr. Brassfield prepared to go back inside the school. Wishbone was ready to trot along right behind him.

It's about time. Lead me to the computers, Wishbone thought.

Mr. Brassfield turned around and looked at Wishbone. "Get away from here," he said. "Scat!"

"*Scat?* Who do you think you're talking to, anyway? A cat?"

Mr. Brassfield ducked inside, and the door swung shut behind him.

"Hey, you can't shut me out! Obviously, you don't know who you're dealing with! I have three good friends in there. They come to school here every day!"

The door didn't move, and Mr. Brassfield didn't come back. No one came. The door remained shut tight. Wishbone put his nose to the crack at the bottom and sniffed. He was good at sniffing out adventure, but he could smell other things, as well. He could smell chalk dust and the cold air of the building's air-conditioning system. He could smell leftover meat loaf from the cafeteria.

And he could smell his friends.

"I know you're in there. I can smell you."

Wishbone scratched at the door again. His nails clicked against the metal. There was no response from the other side of the door. Wishbone finally made his way back to the sidewalk and sat there, staring at the school building. He was very disappointed to be shut out of something he wanted so much to be a part of. The warm sun felt good on his black-and-white coat, but Wishbone was feeling sad.

"Joe? Sam? David? I want to be inside with the three of you guys. Please, don't shut me out."

Wishbone's situation reminded him of a character named D'Artagnan. He was a young man who desperately wanted to be one of the king's musketeers, the highly respected group of special guards, in the famous novel *The Three Musketeers*.

The Three Musketeers was written by Alexandre Dumas and published in France in 1844. It's a great story about courage, sword-fighting, and friendship. And it all starts with a young man with a dream. . . .

Chapter Two

*W*ishbone imagined that *he* was D'Artagnan, living in France in the 1600s. He was young and filled with the spirit of adventure. D'Artagnan lived in the French farming province of Gascony. He was determined, however, to go to the big city of Paris, which was north of his home. In Paris, he would do his best to become a musketeer, one of the men whose duty it was to serve France by protecting the king and his royal circle of people.

D'Artagnan's father was in full agreement with his son's desire. "I have taught you well the art of the sword," his father said on the day D'Artagnan was to leave the countryside and head for the French capital. "You are quick and graceful, and you are strong. Never fear quarrels, and always seek adventures."

D'Artagnan's whiskers twitched with excitement. "Adventure is my middle name. I can hardly wait to get started!"

"And remember," his father continued, "take insults from no one, and always have courage. It is by courage alone that a man can make his way in the world."

"I will remember your teachings well," D'Artagnan

said. He was so excited he felt chills running up and down his fur.

"I am sure you will," his father said. He held out his own sword, along with a letter of introduction to Monsieur Tréville, the captain of the highly respected musketeers. Then, his father put the letter in D'Artagnan's satchel and strapped the sword on his son. "Monsieur Tréville was my good friend when we were youngsters. This letter will introduce you to him and help to gain you a place in his elite command."

Then they went outside their simple house to where D'Artagnan's horse was waiting to carry him off. The animal was, in fact, quite old, without a single hair on its tail. The beast was a strange yellow color. To young D'Artagnan's sensitive nose, the animal smelled quite odd. D'Artagnan leaped to the top of a barrel, and from there he sprang into the saddle, taking the reins tightly into his mouth. He and his father exchanged farewells, and then D'Artagnan trotted off into the distance.

He smelled the sweet scent of the fresh country air, and he felt the wind rustle against his fur. His sense of excitement grew every moment. Big things were about to happen for him; he was sure of it.

When D'Artagnan came to the small town of Meung, he stopped outside a country inn to water the poor nag at a trough. At the doorway of the inn, a number of men gathered. One of them laughed in a manner that D'Artagnan found disrespectful. Remembering his father's words about insults and courage, D'Artagnan left his horse to drink, while he walked toward the men.

"I do not suppose that you are laughing at me," he said, dusting off his simple, crudely woven clothes.

The man was wearing a velvet doublet, a close-fitting jacket. He had an ugly scar that ran from the corner of one eye past his mouth and halfway down his chin. He smiled unpleasantly and stepped forward.

"I was not laughing at you," he said. "I was laughing at your yellow horse, and at your poor country clothes."

The man's mocking tone made D'Artagnan angry. He reached back with his mouth and drew his sword part of the way from its sheath. "A man who insults my horse might also insult me," he said. *"En garde!"*

Okay, sword-fighting fans: "En garde" is a phrase that fencers call out to warn their opponents to get into a fighting position. It means "get ready to fight."

The man with the scar drew his own sword, as D'Artagnan took his sword in his paw. Instantly, the pair was engaged in a heated duel. Their heavy swords clanged together. As the men moved this way and that, the dust of the inn's yard whirled about their feet.

D'Artagnan's weighty blade darted in and out like a hummingbird. He soon gained the advantage in the fight. Several chickens that happened to be in the way scattered wildly, clucking loudly and flapping their wings so that feathers flew.

The scarred man's companions began to realize that their friend was going to be defeated by the young man from the countryside. The scarred man's friends had no swords of their own, so they decided to come to the aid of their friend by picking up sticks and rocks to heave at D'Artagnan.

"Cowards!" D'Artagnan yelled. He dodged the sticks and rocks that pelted him. However, some of the missiles struck him, and he could feel their painful sting against his fur and hide. "If you cannot join in a fair fight, you should not fight at all."

The others were not to be stopped, however. They

continued to throw rocks and sticks at D'Artagnan as
their friend kept on thrusting with his sword. D'Artagnan
knew he needed to do something, and quickly. He
leaped across the water trough, ran behind one of his
opponents, and jabbed him in the rear with the point
of his sword. The man yelled and pitched forward face-
first into the water trough, where D'Artagnan's yellow
horse continued to drink calmly.

"Apologize for your bad behavior, and I will let
you live!" D'Artagnan shouted to the scarred man.

"Never!" the man shot back, just as D'Artagnan's
sword sliced through the man's short velvet jacket.
"And I will make you regret tearing my clothing!"

"Tearing your clothes?" D'Artagnan repeated.
"You're just lucky I didn't tear *you!*"

The man made a savage thrust with his sword, but
D'Artagnan nimbly sidestepped the attack. Seeing that

the man had left himself open to more harm, D'Artagnan was about to plunge his blade into the man's side. Suddenly, a large rock struck D'Artagnan solidly on his paw and caused him to drop his sword. The scarred man's friends jumped on D'Artagnan and held him tightly as he struggled to get free.

"Good work," the scarred man said to the one who had heaved the big rock. "Now, let us see who this hot-headed youngster is."

He searched through D'Artagnan's clothing and soon discovered the letter of introduction addressed to Monsieur Tréville.

"The musketeers are always making trouble for me," he said angrily. "I will just keep this letter for myself."

"You will be sorry if you do, *monsieur*," warned D'Artagnan.

"I doubt that," the man replied.

As the scar-faced man was tucking the letter away safely in his clothing, a coach rolled to a stop at the inn's front yard. The man walked over to it and began to speak to the woman passenger who sat inside.

D'Artagnan was still held tightly in the grip of the cowards who had thrown sticks and rocks at him. Each of the men held one of D'Artagnan's paws, making it impossible for him to move. They made no attempt to cover his eyes to prevent him from seeing what was going on.

D'Artagnan saw the stranger and the woman engaged in conversation. The woman did not look anything like the plain, simple farm girls whom D'Artagnan was accustomed to seeing in Gascony. She was, in fact, quite beautiful, with pale skin and long golden curls and sky-blue eyes. D'Artagnan's keen ears perked up as he attempted to hear what was being said by the pair at the coach, but the only word he caught was the name "Milady." He struggled to get free, pushing away a hand with his nose.

"Watch it!" the scar-faced man yelled. "He's trying to get away! Let's lock him up."

They carried D'Artagnan inside and bribed the innkeeper to lock him up in the wine cellar.

A while later, when the innkeeper had released D'Artagnan, the man with the scar and his friends were long gone.

"I am sorry, *monsieur*," the innkeeper apologized. "Those men paid me to lock you up. They would have harmed me if I had not cooperated with their demand."

D'Artagnan accepted the apology and went outside to seek his sword. It still lay in the dust near the trough. Taking the sword in his mouth, he wiped it carefully against his clothes.

"Someday that scarred fellow and I will meet again," D'Artagnan said. He growled and shook his head. "And then he will be sorry for stealing my letter. Now I will have to introduce myself to Monsieur Treville without a written recommendation."

He walked over to his yellow horse and sighed at the sight of the old nag. He would find a better horse once he arrived in Paris. Then he jumped up onto the rim of the water trough; from there, he leaped into the saddle and urged his horse forward.

It was not in D'Artagnan's nature to be angry or regretful for long. He might have no letter, but he still had his fine sword and his positive outlook. One way or another, he was determined to become a musketeer.

Helllooo! Welcome to . . .

Wishbone's Official Dictionary of Fencing and French Words You May Not Know.

This is where I will explain words used to describe sword-fighting in this book, and French words you will see. Try not to get the French words and the fencing terms confused—you don't want to get into a sword fight when you're just trying to say "good morning"!

FENCING TERMS

en garde: "get ready." This is a warning called out to an opponent to take a fighting stance to defend himself right before a duel begins.

hilt: handle of a sword

lunge: a thrust with a sword. This move is an attack.

parry: to ward off, turn aside, or evade a thrust. This is a defensive move.

pommel: a rounded knob on the hilt, or handle, of a sword

rapier: a long, lightweight sword used for fencing

riposte: a quick thrust given after parrying a lunge. This is a counterattack.

sheath: a case for a sword. *To sheathe* a sword means to put it in its sheath.

thrust: to push a sword forward with force, or to stab. This move is an attack.

FRENCH TERMS

bonjour: good morning; good day

carte blanche: a written document that gives someone the freedom to do anything at any time, without any penalty

fleur-de-lis: "lily flower." The lily-flower mark was sometimes branded (or burned) onto the skin of criminals who were scheduled for execution.

moi: me

mon ami: my friend; my pal

monsieur: Mr.; sir

quel dommage: what a pity

Chapter Three

*D'*Artagnan arrived in the city of Paris for the very first time in the year 1625. In those days, the city was torn between two opposing leaders, and each one wanted all the power for himself. One was Cardinal Richelieu, a man of great importance in the Church. The other one was King Louis XIII, who was served most loyally by his personal guards—the highly trained and skilled musketeers.

The musketeers, of course, were the Good Guys, and D'Artagnan was going to join their ranks. Not that it was going to be easy to do so; they didn't accept just anybody into their select circle. But D'Artagnan had the dogged determination (the very best kind of determination, naturally) to become the greatest musketeer of them all!

The city of Paris fascinated D'Artagnan. He had seen nothing like it in his rural hometown in Gascony. He had never even imagined such a wonderful place. People were bustling almost everywhere along magnificent tree-lined boulevards, and many of the citizens were dressed elegantly in the latest fashions. Other townspeople were obviously poor, without even enough money to buy shoes for their feet.

The avenues were wide, with plenty of room for carts and horse-drawn carriages to pass up and down. D'Artagnan could smell the earthy aroma of the horses that pulled the carriages. He sniffed at the smoke that rose up through chimneys from wood fires, where all sorts of food was being cooked in the houses that lined the streets. The intoxicating scent of freshly baked bread mingled with the aroma of roasting lamb. All of these heavenly odors made D'Artagnan's mouth water, and he licked his chops at the thought of a great meal.

D'Artagnan was not intimidated by the sophisticated city-dwellers. He, too, fancied himself to be quite clever and dashing, even in his rough country clothes. He was also quick and resourceful, and he believed that he could hold his own with anyone.

He trotted down a busy street until he stood in front of a heavy wooden gate. The sign posted on the gate read: L'HÔTEL DE TRÉVILLE. D'Artagnan knew that this was the barracks where the musketeers lived and trained. Although he no longer had his letter of introduction, he did not hesitate to go forward. Pushing off on his hind legs, he jumped straight in the air, grabbed the bell rope with his teeth, and gave it a good tug.

"Open up in there! The newest musketeer is here!" D'Artagnan called.

The gate swung open at the tinkling of the bell, and D'Artagnan stepped into the courtyard.

"All right," he said. "Here I am, musketeers! I'm rough! I'm tough! I'm . . . wow!" D'Artagnan was not easily impressed; however, what he saw before him in the courtyard was pretty overwhelming. There were men everywhere, most of them wearing the colorful garb of the musketeers—blue capes and gold crosses and feathered hats.

Their swords flashed and rang out loudly and glinted in the bright sunshine as they practiced different fencing moves with one another. D'Artagnan had never seen men so skilled and dashing. To them, fencing was both a duty *and* a pleasure. The men's smiling faces reflected the pride and satisfaction they had in their great sword-fighting abilities.

One spirited trainee stepped backward up a stone staircase as he crossed swords with a man who pressed him ever upward. The blades chimed and echoed like bells. D'Artagnan thought the man might trip, but he didn't.

D'Artagnan wasn't sure exactly what to do. Then he decided that perhaps he should simply join right in with the fun.

"En garde!" he said to himself.

D'Artagnan drew his sword and ran over to where the man was dueling on the staircase. The man looked as if he could use some help, but D'Artagnan got there a bit late to pitch in. The man flipped his opponent's sword into the air, caught it by the pommel as it came down, then handed it to his friend with a laugh.

Wow! These guys are really good, D'Artagnan thought.

The agile swordsman did not laugh for long, however. His merriment ceased entirely when he stepped off the stairway. He stopped smiling completely. Wondering what was wrong, D'Artagnan failed to get out of the man's way in time, and the musketeer stumbled over him. The swordsman fell forward for several feet, flailing his arms wildly and trying desperately not to fall smack on his face.

"Pardon me," D'Artagnan said, dashing aside to get out of his way.

"Pardon, indeed," the man responded when he finally came to a halt. "You clumsy wag. How dare you?"

It was only an accident, and perhaps the man did not mean to be insulting. D'Artagnan tried to control his temper. "Wag?" he repeated. "I'll have you know that I wasn't wagging a thing!"

"You deliberately stood in my way," the swordsman said accusingly. "You were trying to make me look foolish."

"I ask your pardon once again," D'Artagnan replied, gritting his teeth.

"You ask my pardon?" the man said with a sneer. "You embarrass a musketeer, and all you can say is that you ask my pardon? You need a lesson in manners, you insolent youngster, and I'm just the one to give it to you. I challenge you to a duel at noon tomorrow, near the building called Carmes-Deschaux."

Insolent? D'Artagnan thought. *Who's being insolent? This guy is really asking for it!*

"A duel?" D'Artagnan said aloud, pleased at the idea. He wagged his tail for emphasis. "Fine. I'll be there, and we'll just see who learns a lesson."

The man snorted, then moved away. D'Artagnan turned his attention to another man. This one was stout, obviously well fed. He was talking loudly with some women who laughed at his chatter.

Now, here's a musketeer who knows how to have fun, D'Artagnan thought. He heard the women exclaiming about the man's clothing, which indeed was very fine.

"A man who dresses well will always have an advantage," the rotund man said. "I myself wear only

23

the very best clothing. My tailor is superior to any other one in Paris."

He's certainly proud of his appearance, D'Artagnan thought. *But what's this?* As he approached the laughing man, D'Artagnan noticed that a bit of fabric hung loose from the man's otherwise elegant royal blue cape. D'Artagnan was sure that such a dangling thread could be embarrassing to a man who took such pride in his outfit. He decided to run over and help.

Unfortunately, D'Artagnan was just a little too eager, and running just a little too fast. So, instead of helping, he got tangled up in the cape. Struggling to get free, D'Artagnan accidentally pulled the cape tightly around its owner's neck, almost choking him.

"*Ga-a-a-ck!*" the man gurgled. His clever conversation with the women was cut short as his face reddened and he strained for breath. The man jerked at his cape. There was a loud ripping noise as he finally succeeded in freeing his neck. He gasped in deep mouthfuls of air.

At the same time, D'Artagnan struggled with the cape. His teeth were sunken into the plush cloth, and a large portion of it tore away.

Regaining his breath, the man glared down at D'Artagnan. "Are you trying to ambush me?"

"Ambush you?" D'Artagnan said. "How could I ambush anyone with this cape in my mouth?" D'Artagnan spat out the piece of cape. "I was only trying to help."

The man was not pleased. "Help? By destroying my cape? It is—it *was*—quite valuable, but look at it now! You are impudent and discourteous!"

"I was only trying to help. I don't think you understand."

"You think that I, a musketeer, do not understand? What I understand—perfectly well—is that my cloak is ripped to shreds, and it is entirely your fault. If there is more to know, perhaps you will be so kind as to enlighten me—in a duel, tomorrow at noon!"

All right! D'Artagnan thought. *Duel number two! This is getting better and better! If that's what you want, you've got it, pal.*

But there was a slight problem. "Sorry," said D'Artagnan. "I'm already booked for noon. Would one o'clock suit you?"

"One o'clock it is, near the large building called Carmes-Deschaux."

D'Artagnan held out his paw to shake on it.

The good news was that D'Artagnan wouldn't have far to walk between duels. However, his experience so far at Monsieur Tréville's training academy wasn't going exactly as he'd planned.

D'Artagnan had hoped to make an impression on the musketeers, and he certainly had. He'd come to Paris for excitement, and he had definitely found it. But he wanted to fit in, to be part of the group, to prove he was worthy of serving among the honorable musketeers. He did not want to become number one on their hit list. And he definitely did not want to make them run him through with their swords.

D'Artagnan looked around for someone who might be more friendly than those whom he had met so far.

He saw a musketeer in quiet conversation with two other musketeers. The man was dressed differently from everyone else; he wore all black. As he spoke, he made a gesture with his hands. In doing so, he dislodged something that had been stuck casually into one of his pockets.

D'Artagnan saw that the object was a lace

handkerchief, and it fluttered to the ground. The speaker seemed not to notice, and he covered the delicate handkerchief with his heavy boot.

D'Artagnan ran over and took the edge of the handkerchief between his teeth. He tugged on the delicate lace, wagging his head from side to side and pushing back with all four paws. Still, the handkerchief didn't budge from beneath the man's boot.

Noticing D'Artagnan's efforts, the man cried out, in an angry tone, "Stop that!"

D'Artagnan released the lace at once. "Sir, you are dirtying a delicate handkerchief that must belong to a fine lady."

The man looked down but pretended not to see the handkerchief. He said to his friends, "May I have a moment alone with this annoying youth?"

Annoying? D'Artagnan thought. *This guy is really asking for it!*

As the musketeer's friends moved away, he frowned at D'Artagnan. "I am showing a lot of patience with you because I am studying to be a priest someday.

Now listen to me carefully, young man. Sometimes one steps on a handkerchief for a very good reason."

The musketeer looked around to see where his friends were. When he saw that they were off to the side, busy talking to one another, he quickly moved his booted foot, reached down subtlely, and picked up the handkerchief. He then quickly tucked it away inside his cloak.

"But what would be a good reason for stepping on such a pretty handkerchief? You're getting it all dirty."

The musketeer said, "Why, you unmannerly clod! You dare to speak in such a way to a musketeer?"

"You can't think of any reason, can you?" said D'Artagnan. "Does it belong to your girlfriend?" he asked teasingly.

The musketeer glared at D'Artagnan. "You have no understanding of honor. Your behavior is totally unacceptable," said the musketeer angrily.

"Honor?" D'Artagnan repeated. "Unacceptable behavior? Look who's talking! I'm not the one who stepped on my girlfriend's hanky."

The musketeer gave D'Artagnan a piercing stare and said, "I will listen to no more of your backtalk. I challenge you to a duel. Meet me tomorrow near the abbey Carmes-Deschaux at two o'clock." Then he immediately turned on his heel and stomped away, entering a building off the courtyard.

Wow! Three duels in one day! Talk about being booked solid! D'Artagnan thought. *And I've been in Paris only a few hours! I wonder if I'm setting some kind of a record. I'm famous already. I'm sure my father would be proud of me!*

Paris was going to be as thrilling as D'Artagnan had always expected it would be. *En garde!*

Chapter Four

Joe was standing with Sam and David by the computer in the science lab. Mr. Delgado, a handsome man with black hair and a ready smile, came rolling up to them in his wheelchair. Joe liked him and knew he was one of the most popular teachers in the school. Mr. Delgado was cradling a CD in his lap as he wheeled himself along.

"Okay, kids," Mr. Delgado said, showing them the CD. "This is it. Wait till I show you what's on this. Once you've seen the beauty of fractal geometry, you'll understand how mathematics can also be art."

"Great!" Joe said. He wasn't exactly sure what fractal geometry was, but he had heard great things about this CD-ROM. Joe pushed the button that opened the CD-ROM holder, and Mr. Delgado inserted the CD. Joe pushed the button again, and the CD holder slid smoothly back into the computer case.

Music began to play from the computer's stereo speakers. A picture flashed onto the view screen. But before Joe or anyone else had a chance to see what it was, the music died out. There was a popping noise, and then suddenly the monitor went blank.

"What happened?" Mr. Delgado asked.

"I think the computer crashed," Sam told him.

"But that can't be," Mr. Delgado said. "It was working fine only a little while ago."

David, who knew quite a bit about computers, said, "Your port connections must be bad, then."

"That's probably what it is," Joe said. Then he followed the computer's power cord with his eyes. "Uh-oh. I think I've found the trouble."

Mr. Delgado turned in his chair. "Trouble? I don't like the sound of that."

Joe bent down to reach something on the floor. When he stood up, he was holding the power cord, which was frayed and ragged. "Look at this."

"It looks like something chewed on it," Sam said. "What would do a thing like that?"

Mr. Delgado sighed. "Mort," he said.

Joe dropped the cord. "Mort?"

"Mort, the lab rat?" Sam asked.

Mr. Delgado nodded. "That's right. Good old Mort."

"How did he get in here?" David asked. "I thought he was kept in a cage."

"He was," Mr. Delgado said. "But somehow he got out. He's been on the loose for about a week now. He's chewed up half the school, and he's got to be stopped."

Wishbone trotted along in back of the school building until he came to a large riding lawn mower and a rack of bicycles.

"This place looks as secure as a fortress, but Stealth Dog can always find a weak spot," Wishbone said.

There were several cardboard boxes stacked against the red-brick wall of the building. About a foot above the boxes, there was a window propped open with a short piece of wood.

"Ah-ha! Helll-o-o-o, open window! Stealth Dog triumphs again!"

Wishbone headed for the stack of boxes, ready to climb them and slip inside the building. Suddenly he saw something moving on the window ledge. It was something white, with beady eyes, stiff whiskers, and a twitchy nose. The "something" looked like . . .

". . . a rat! They let a rat inside the school, but not a cute little dog? Now, isn't that just fine! What *is* the world coming to?"

Wishbone stared at the rat, who stared at Wishbone with his black, oil-drop eyes for a moment. Then, with a flick of his tail, the rat disappeared into the school building.

Wishbone didn't let the sight of the rat bother him. He ran right up the stack of boxes as if it were a flight of steps.

"There's my opening. Stealth Dog discovers the secret entrance, and he is about to enter the building undetected!"

Reaching the top of the stack of boxes, Wishbone realized that he still could not quite reach the open window.

"Stealth Dog leaps!"

Wishbone jumped toward the window opening. As he passed through it, his legs dislodged the piece of wood that propped open the window, and it slammed shut behind him. Wishbone plunged downward into the unknown.

"Ya-a-a-a-a-ah!"

The disoriented dog landed on all fours with a muffled thud and found himself in near darkness. Soft, papery things were crowding in on him from all sides: top, bottom, left, and right. It took a moment for Wishbone to realize he had landed in a box of toilet-paper rolls. Wishbone righted himself and stood on his hind legs to peer over the edge of the box.

Surveying his surroundings, he saw a concrete floor, and a sink off to one side. Standing all around were pails, mops, push-brooms, tools, and colorful plastic bottles.

Wishbone sniffed the air. He could smell soap, oil, disinfectant, and even a slight hint of meat loaf.

"Something tells me this isn't the executive suite," he said.

Leaning carefully against the side of the box, Wishbone rocked back and forth until he finally tipped it over and tumbled out onto the floor, bumping his

head. He was followed by numerous rolls of toilet paper, some of which began unraveling themselves before he could stop them.

Wishbone sat up and shook his head. "This must be Mr. Brassfield's workroom. I don't think I'll find any CD-ROMs in here."

Glancing to his left, Wishbone saw that the door to the room was closed. He trotted over to the door and pushed at it with his nose. It didn't budge.

"Stealth Dog has to find a way to get to the computer lab," Wishbone said.

Well, at least I've accomplished Step 1 in my quest—I've actually made my way *into* the school building. I just hope I haven't bitten off more than I can chew, so to speak, the way D'Artagnan did in setting up those three duels.

Chapter Five

D'Artagnan knew that scheduling three duels in one afternoon was foolhardy. The fact that they would come one right after the other made the whole situation even more dangerous. But he was young and brave, and he was more than willing to fight to defend his honor.

He had left Paris in plenty of time to get to the duels. He came trotting out of the woods and crossed a little bridge near a large building called Carmes-Deschaux. D'Artagnan knew the building was an abbey, where religious people lived and studied. The white walls of the abbey glistened in the noonday sun, and birds sang in the trees. A squirrel chattered nearby, but D'Artagnan would not be distracted from the task at hand by the pleasures of the chase. The water of a little brook whispered as it trickled under the bridge.

In short, it was a lovely day, just right for adventure and excitement. Near the abbey stood the musketeer with whom D'Artagnan had scheduled the first duel. The man wore a very serious expression, as if he were thinking deeply about something.

Well, D'Artagnan thought, *now I'll find out if my bite lives up to my bark.*

"*Bonjour, monsieur*," D'Artagnan said. "Am I late?"

The musketeer waved a hand. "No, no. You are not late. I am early, and my seconds—my assistants—have not yet arrived. Permit me to introduce myself. My name is Athos."

Athos was resting against a low, stone wall. D'Artagnan took a moment to jump up on the wall. He sat beside Athos and wagged his tail politely.

"And I am D'Artagnan. I am pleased to make your acquaintance, even under these circumstances."

Just as D'Artagnan finished speaking, two men approached.

"Ah," said Athos. "Here are my seconds. The one dressed all in black is Aramis. The other is my good friend Porthos."

D'Artagnan stared at the two men in surprise. He recognized both of them, of course. He was supposed to fight duels with each of them later that very afternoon.

The musketeers recognized D'Artagnan, as well. Porthos said, "Why, I am supposed to fight this young fellow at one o'clock!"

"And I," Aramis said, "have a duel scheduled with him at two!"

"That is your misfortune," said Athos with the hint of a smile. "I am to fight him first. That means he will likely be unable to keep his appointments with the two of you."

Athos gestured to D'Artagnan.

"Are you ready?" Athos asked.

Am I ready? I was born *ready!* D'Artagnan

thought. Aloud, he said, "First, I must offer my apologies to you, Monsieur Porthos, and also to you, Monsieur Aramis."

The musketeers laughed.

But D'Artagnan said, "I'm afraid that you don't understand me. I am not trying to avoid the duels. On the contrary—I am eagerly looking forward to them. But if Monsieur Athos kills me first, I will not be available to fight you two. I merely ask you to excuse me on that account."

Athos looked thoughtfully at D'Artagnan. Then he whisked out his sword from its hilt and slashed to his left and then to his right. The sword sparkled in the sunlight as he tested it.

"I want you to know," Athos said to D'Artagnan, "that I admire your courage. It is plain to see that you have a noble heart. Under different circumstances, we might have become friends. But I suppose that is not to be. Shall we begin?"

D'Artagnan reached back with his mouth and drew his sword, which he quickly took in one paw. Crossing his sword with that of Athos, he said, "I await your orders."

Their swords had hardly clashed when five men arrived on the scene. They were all dressed in the red-and-white uniforms of Cardinal Richelieu's guards.

"Richelieu's men!" Athos cried. "Sheathe your swords quickly, gentlemen!"

It was too late for that, however. The positions of D'Artagnan and Athos made their intention to duel all too clear to any observer.

"Greetings, musketeers," the leader of the cardinal's guards said. He was a solidly built man with a thick black moustache. "It appears that you are engaged in a

duel. I must assume you are also aware that His Eminence, Cardinal Richelieu, has issued an order that expressly forbids dueling. I command you to stop in his name!"

"Stop?" Athos replied. "I assure you that if we were to see you fighting, we would not try to stop you. In any case, our loyalty is to His Majesty the King. Go now, and leave us alone to conduct our own affairs."

"I cannot leave without first performing my duty," the leader said. "Put up your swords and follow me."

"They will not," Porthos said. "And we will not be told what to do by Richelieu's flunkies."

The leader of the cardinal's guards frowned beneath his moustache. "Flunkies, you say?"

"Indeed, we do," Aramis told him. "Flunkies. Or hirelings. Or would you rather be called the cardinal's toadies?"

Athos laughed. "But whatever name you prefer, take yourselves away from here. We have important business to conduct."

The musketeer's scornful tone angered the leader of the cardinal's guards. "If you will not obey our command, we will be forced to arrest you."

"There are five of them," Athos said, "and only three of us musketeers. But I swear that I will die upon this very spot before I disgrace the musketeers."

Porthos and Aramis stepped closer to Athos as he spoke. Meanwhile, the cardinal's guards grouped themselves together. D'Artagnan knew that he had to make a choice. If he fought on the side of the musketeers, he would make an enemy of the cardinal. Once he gave his loyalty to a particular group, he could not take it back.

Yet D'Artagnan did not hesitate even for a fraction

of a second. After all, was he not already a musketeer because of his loyalty, if he was not one in name? He could feel it deep down in his fur.

"Gentlemen," D'Artagnan said, "I believe there is some mistake. Monsieur Athos said there were only three of us. I make it four."

"You are not one of us," Porthos said. "This is not your fight."

"It is true that I am not officially one of you, but I have the heart of a musketeer, gentlemen, and that heart persuades me to fight on your side."

"You do indeed have a noble heart," Athos said. "It is just as I perceived. But we may die here, you know."

"I am aware of that, *monsieur*, but I am prepared to fight. I am not afraid. Now, let me prove it to you."

"What is all this blather?" yelled the leader of the cardinal's guards. "Will you obey my order, or will you fight?"

"It appears that we will fight," Aramis said, as he and Porthos whipped out their swords.

D'Artagnan growled deep in his throat, and the fur stood up on the back of his neck. Honor! Courage! This was what being a member of the musketeers was all about!

The guards snatched out their rapiers in reply, and the nine combatants charged one another with furious cries, and flashing and clanging swords.

Chapter Six

*W*hen the battle began, D'Artagnan barked with joy, jumped up in the air, and wagged his tail. He was elated to find himself matched against none other than the leader of Cardinal Richelieu's guards. The man's name was Jussac, and he was reported to be one of the most skilled swordsmen among the guards.

Nothing like starting off with the best, D'Artagnan thought. He ducked and then popped up around Jussac, darting in and out, matching the guard's sword stroke for stroke. He thrust with such speed that his blade was a long silver blur. And with four feet, D'Artagnan knew his footwork was unbeatable. Poor Jussac must have thought he was being attacked by ten swordsmen at once.

D'Artagnan hardly had time to glance around to see how his comrades were doing. Out of the corner of his eye, however, he noticed that Porthos and Athos were fighting one man each. Aramis was busy fending off the remaining two. D'Artagnan would have liked to help Aramis against the uneven odds, but he was too busy with his own duel. D'Artagnan bobbed and dodged and parried all of Jussac's thrusts. He made stinging hits on both of the guardsman's arms. Each time the sword point touched Jussac, the man cried out loudly.

"Just be glad that I'm taking it easy on you," D'Artagnan said as he continued his all-out assault on Jussac. "I'm only warming up."

D'Artagnan was so quick and agile with his blade that Jussac was unable to give him so much as a scratch.

"Enough!" Jussac shouted at the energetic D'Artagnan. "Stand still, and I will run you through!"

D'Artagnan ignored Jussac's threats and continued to attack him from every angle. Jussac spun around each time and defended himself.

Don't sneak up behind me, D'Artagnan thought. *There will be absolutely no back-stabbing in this duel!*

D'Artagnan's extra energy and four strong feet gave his opponent reason to pause. Jussac made serious mistakes in his attacks, leaving too many openings for D'Artagnan's swift sword.

Thinking that he had caught D'Artagnan off guard, Jussac leaped forward and aimed a powerful thrust right at his opponent's heart. But D'Artagnan jumped aside easily. Then he parried the thrust, and Jussac's pointed blade slipped safely past him. With his own sword held firmly, D'Artagnan plunged it into Jussac's unprotected side. Jussac dropped his weapon and fell to the ground, injured.

"Now to help my friends," D'Artagnan said.

Aramis and Porthos were fighting fiercely. They seemed to have the contest going in their favor. Athos, on the other hand, was not faring very well at all. He was wounded in two places, and his face was very pale.

Even worse, his right arm appeared to be useless. He had been forced to switch his sword to his left hand. It was clear he was having a lot of difficulty.

Athos gave D'Artagnan a look that showed his need for help, even if the musketeer's pride would never allow him to ask out loud for it. He would have died first.

D'Artagnan sprang to Athos's side and snarled at the guardsman. "I pray you, pick on someone who is not wounded, *monsieur.*"

Athos, who had been supported by nothing more than his courage, sank to his knees. The guardsman then turned his attention to D'Artagnan.

Athos called out to D'Artagnan, "Do not kill him. I will settle the score with him in a moment, as soon as I catch my breath."

D'Artagnan engaged the guardsman with a rapid thrust. As his new enemy attempted to parry, brave D'Artagnan twirled his own blade around the guardsman's blade in a rapid, ringing circle. The man's mouth dropped open in surprise as his sword was knocked from his hand. He watched it soar through the air like a javelin to land fifty feet away.

"Well done!" Athos called out. "Well done!"

D'Artagnan and the guardsman both raced to claim the sword. D'Artagnan had three advantages: he was faster, more agile, and closer to the ground. He dashed to the sword and grabbed it in his teeth.

The guardsman was not dismayed. He ran to the man Aramis had wounded and borrowed his sword. By that time, Athos had recovered enough to stand and fight again.

"I have caught my breath," Athos called out. D'Artagnan knew that Athos would not need any help now. He watched the musketeer and the guardsman thrust, parry, and riposte until suddenly the guardsman fell.

By the way, fencing fans, here's a quick refresher course in swordplay terminology. ***Thrust*** **means to poke your opponent with your sword.** ***Parry*** **means to block a blow. And** *riposte* **means to retaliate after a parry.**

Once D'Artagnan saw that Athos was victorious, he looked over to Aramis. He was standing over the second of his fallen foes. Aramis had his sword point right at the man's throat. "Ask for mercy," Aramis said, "and you may yet escape with your life."

The man begged for his life, and Aramis moved the point of his sword aside. Meanwhile, Porthos was still fighting. He teased his opponent in the hopes of gaining an advantage.

"What time do you think it is?" Porthos said. "Time for your afternoon nap?"

The man did not respond.

Porthos continued his verbal assault. "How do you like my outfit? My tailor is the finest in all of Europe. Do I not look handsome?"

There was no response to that remark, either. However, Porthos had managed to distract his opponent just enough to slip under his guard and poke him in the arm with the point of his sword. The man fell heavily to the ground.

"It's time to admit defeat," Athos said to Jussac.

Jussac glared at the musketeer. He struggled to his feet, and he and his wounded men left the field in front of the abbey. As the cardinal's guards hobbled away, the musketeers gathered up their swords.

After they had picked up their equipment, Athos

turned to D'Artagnan. "That was excellent fighting, my young friend."

D'Artagnan cried out happily, "I know I am not yet worthy to be a musketeer, but will you at least allow me to serve as your apprentice—your student?"

"You will not only be our apprentice," said Aramis, "but our friend, as well."

Porthos smiled. "We will groom you for service as a musketeer, and we will teach you all of our best tricks."

"*Fantastique,* to both of your offers," D'Artagnan said. "I could sure use some grooming after all this messy fighting. And even though I know plenty of tricks already, it's never too late to learn a few new ones."

Athos said, "Porthos, Aramis, and I are known far and wide as the three inseparables. You, D'Artagnan, will become the fourth member of our special club."

"All for one, and one for all!" D'Artagnan said. "Shall we make that our motto?"

"An excellent idea," Athos agreed. "Let us put out our hands in agreement."

The musketeers extended their hands one by one, and D'Artagnan's paw landed right on top.

"All for one, and one for all!" the musketeers and D'Artagnan shouted together.

That's a wonderful motto. I hope my friends Joe, David, and Samantha know that I feel the same way about them as D'Artagnan feels about his buddies. Which reminds me—I'd better go nose around and find Joe, Sam, and David. They might need protection from that rat!

43

Chapter Seven

*W*ishbone sniffed at the crack under the closed door. He could smell floor cleaner and rubber from the soles of many sneakers. He got another whiff of the meat loaf from the cafeteria. But he could no longer pick up the scent of his friends.

He turned to survey the room. There was no sign of the rat, so Wishbone began sniffing around the mops and brooms. "Stealth Dog looks for the scent. I smell soap and water. I smell dust. I smell . . . a rat!"

Wishbone's head jerked up, and his sharp eyes looked all around. Not a creature was stirring, not even a mouse—much less a rat.

"I know you're in here," Wishbone growled. "I don't know where you're hiding, but Stealth Dog always gets his man . . . er . . . his rat. You might as well give up and come on out."

The rat, if he was there, didn't make a sound. Wishbone began to make a full circuit of the room, sniffing everything in sight.

There was no response from the rat.

"Fine. Just keep quiet. I didn't want to talk to you anyway."

Wishbone sniffed a shovel. He smelled mud and grass, but nothing else. He caught a scent from an overturned box.

"Nice smell! What could it be? . . . Oh, it's me! That's the box *I* was in."

Wishbone walked around the box. There was nothing behind it except some rolls of toilet paper that were mostly unraveled.

"He must be the Houdini of the rat world. I don't know how else he could have disappeared so completely."

Suddenly, there was a noise in the hallway, and Wishbone's ears stood up. He ran to the door to listen.

"Well," he heard Mr. Delgado say on the other side of the door, "That rat, Mort, is costing us money by destroying school property."

That's Mr. Delgado. And . . . yes! It's Joe! Wishbone thought. "Here I am, buddy. Lemme outta here!" he called.

Then Wishbone heard Mr. Brassfield. "You're right about Mort, Mr. Delgado. And from the looks of this power cord you've given me, I'd say it's past time I put a stop to his little tricks."

Wishbone stood up on his hind legs and leaned against the door with his front paws. "No, no, let *me* get him! I'm the best rodent-catcher in town. Seriously, I really am. Trust me. Even cats come to me for professional advice. I'll show you that you can't run this school without me! You'll never catch that rat without my help!"

"I'd better go to the hardware store," Mr. Brassfield

said on the other side of the door. "It's time to load up with rat traps."

"And we'll go pick up a new power cable for the computer," Joe said. "We can't see that CD-ROM without one."

"Thanks, everybody," Mr. Delgado said. "I'll meet you when you get back."

When Wishbone heard the teacher's chair wheeling away, he said to himself, "I'll find that low-down rat if it's the last thing I do."

He started sniffing again, working his way toward the sink.

The doorknob rattled.

All right! Wishbone thought. *This could be my big chance to escape.*

He turned around. The doorknob rattled again, louder this time.

"This door is stuck," Mr. Brassfield said from the hallway. "It's the third time this week I've had trouble getting it open. I'm going to have to fix that."

He shoved the door harder. Wishbone ran over beside it and stood quietly, waiting for his golden opportunity.

"Gotcha!" Mr. Brassfield said as the door finally swung open. He didn't look down, and Wishbone slipped silently past him into the main hallway of the school.

"They call me . . . Stealth Dog!" he said.

Pausing outside the open door, Wishbone heard Mr. Brassfield say, "I need to get myself organized for the big hunt."

Wishbone peeked around the door frame and saw Mr. Brassfield walk over to a dry erase board that stood near some bookshelves. Locating a piece of chalk, he wrote THINGS I NEED TO DO TODAY on the big board. Then he wrote, in huge capital letters, GET MORT!!!

"Get Mort," Mr. Brassfield said aloud. "And I'm going to do it today."

"If anybody gets Mort, it'll be me," Wishbone said, as he sniffed his way along the hallway, trying to catch a scent of Mort. "Stealth Dog's the name, and rat-catching's my game. Now, let's see. Rats can slip through tiny cracks. Mort probably slipped out of that room even before I did. You can't escape Stealth Dog, Mort. I've got you surrounded. Let me see your beady little eyes."

There was no answer from Mort, who was either shy or not listening. Or maybe he simply wasn't anywhere around.

Wishbone saw an open locker—just the place where a clever rat might hide. Wishbone trotted over to sniff out the situation.

"Hmm . . ." he said, sniffing around the locker. "Someone kept a peanut-butter sandwich in here for a few days. And somebody didn't bother to wash the

soiled gym clothes from last week, either. But I don't smell any rat."

Just then, Wishbone heard a noise above him. Looking up, he saw that Mort was almost directly overhead, scurrying along the tops of the lockers. Wishbone jumped up as high as he could, but he wasn't able to reach the rat.

Well, at least now I'm making some progress in this cat-and-mouse game—uh . . . make that dog-and-rat chase! I wonder if Mort understands that this school isn't big enough for both of us. Pretty soon we'll meet face to face, just as D'Artagnan and Cardinal Richelieu will. . . .

Chapter Eight

D'Artagnan had been in Paris for seven months before he finally met Cardinal Richelieu. He had not yet become a musketeer, but he was by then well known as the constant companion of Athos, Porthos, and Aramis. Word of his adventures had reached the cardinal's interested ears. The cardinal decided that a swordsman with D'Artagnan's superior skills did not belong with the king's guards, but in the red-and-white uniform of the cardinal's guards. The cardinal invited D'Artagnan to an informal meeting.

So, one morning, an usher led D'Artagnan into the room where he was to meet Richelieu. D'Artagnan sniffed cautiously as he entered. At the far end of the room opposite the door through which D'Artagnan entered, there was a large desk and a window that stretched all the way from the floor to the ceiling. The window was hung with heavy, dark curtains, making the light coming into the room quite dim.

"*Bonjour*," D'Artagnan called, peering toward the far end of the room. "Good day. . . . Hey, anybody home?"

A voice from the dimness in back of him said, "Are you D'Artagnan, from Gascony?"

Startled by the speaker, D'Artagnan whipped around as quickly as he did when chasing his own tail. Behind him stood Cardinal Richelieu, a tall man. He was holding a book of some kind in his hands. The cardinal was not old, but his goatee and his moustache were gray, as was the hair on his head. He wore a long scarlet-colored robe that hung down to the floor, and a red cap topped his gray hair. The collar of the robe was of the purest white. Around his neck hung a golden image of the sun on a white cord.

"Cardinal Richelieu," D'Artagnan said, touching his nose to the floor to bow.

The cardinal bobbed his head in return. Then he strode to the far end of the room. "Come along," he said, and D'Artagnan followed.

The cardinal went around the desk and sat in the magnificent high-backed chair that appeared to resemble a throne. The desk was covered with books and manuscripts, and a tall candle stood in a golden candlestick.

"Please," the cardinal said, making a motion with his hand. "Sit down here before me, and we will talk."

D'Artagnan hopped into a velvet-covered chair opposite the cardinal and sat. He waited patiently for the cardinal to speak.

"You have been in Paris for some time now, haven't you?" the cardinal asked. "Seven months, I believe."

D'Artagnan was surprised at the cardinal's knowledge. "Why, yes," he said.

"And," the cardinal continued, "your friendship

with Messieurs Athos, Porthos, and Aramis of the king's musketeers has brought you much adventure in that time, has it not?"

"How did you know?" D'Artagnan wondered. He was puzzled that the cardinal would take such an interest in the activities of someone so new to the city from the countryside.

"It is my business to be aware of all things that happen in Paris," Cardinal Richelieu responded. "I know that you are brave, *monsieur,* but you have created some powerful enemies in the time that you have been here. If you do not take great care, they may very well destroy you."

D'Artagnan didn't like the sound of that remark. He wondered who his enemies were. He was beginning to suspect that the cardinal was one of them. "If I have enemies, what can I do?"

Richelieu folded his hands together atop the desk. "You can choose to serve another master—me. You can wear the red-and-white uniform of the cardinal's guards."

That's it! D'Artagnan thought. *I'm outta here.* He hopped down from the chair, turned his tail on the cardinal, and trotted toward the door.

"Wait," Richelieu called after him.

Rising from his big chair, the cardinal walked along one side of a long table that ran almost the entire length of the room. D'Artagnan was on the other side of the table. The cardinal beat him to the doorway. With his arms crossed on his chest, he stood in front of the door, preventing D'Artagnan's exit.

"I suppose you came to Paris with the idea of making your fortune," the cardinal said.

D'Artagnan had to admit the cardinal was correct.

"That is true. You might say that I'm striving to be Best in Show."

The cardinal smiled. "Serve in my guards. Let me guide you. I can help you reach your goals."

"Sorry to disappoint you, but I'm just not the type to roll over on my friends."

The cardinal's tight smile immediately changed to a look of rage. His face became almost as red as his robe.

"So you are daring to refuse me?" he said, almost in disbelief.

"Please, Your Eminence, try not to take it so personally."

The cardinal's voice turned to ice. He said, *"Quel dommage.* What a pity." He walked stiffly back to his desk. When he reached it, he turned to D'Artagnan and said, "Always remember this, D'Artagnan—if, sometime in the future, you meet with an unfortunate accident, I offered you protection. You are the one who refused to accept it."

The cardinal picked up the bell on his desk and rang it sharply. At the bell's sound, the usher came running and made a skidding stop by the door. The cardinal inclined his head and turned his back on D'Artagnan. He parted the curtains on the enormous window to look outside. D'Artagnan glanced up at the usher, who stood looking straight ahead.

"I can see myself out, thank you," D'Artagnan told the servant.

D'Artagnan stepped into the hallway. He gave a yelp when the door slammed loudly behind him, almost catching his tail. "Hah! I don't think the cardinal approves of me. Well, I'm not exactly wild about him, either."

The hall was lined with statues, but D'Artagnan hardly noticed them.

"How could I be one of the cardinal's guards?" D'Artagnan snorted indignantly. "That's a ridiculous idea if I ever heard one."

"Purrrfectly correct, *monsieur,*" said a woman's voice.

D'Artagnan had been so absorbed in his thoughts that he didn't realize one of the statues was a real person. The woman stepped down from the pedestal where she had been posing motionless and silent.

D'Artagnan was startled, and the fur on his back bristled. "What? Who spoke? Who's there?"

The woman stepped out of the alcove that held the pedestal upon which she had stood. She smiled at D'Artagnan.

"Oh, you're real," D'Artagnan said. "You are so beautiful that at first I thought you were a piece of art."

She wore a long white dress with lace trim at the collar. She had a pearl necklace around her neck, and a high, white-powdered wig on her head.

The beautiful woman smiled coldly. "*Monsieur* is too kind," she said. "And you are quite dashingly handsome yourself."

D'Artagnan was flattered, though he did not say so. Instead, he introduced himself. "I am D'Artagnan."

"Of course," she purred. "I have heard much about you already."

It seems as if everyone knows about me, D'Artagnan thought. *I wonder why they are so interested. True, I am a good fighter. And brave. And loyal. But do those qualities provide enough of a reason for everybody to be sniffing me out, so to speak?*

The beautiful woman scratched D'Artagnan behind his ears. "You may address me as 'Milady.' Now, I have a question for you. May I ask it?"

Milady? D'Artagnan was surprised. He had heard that name often in Paris. In fact, he had heard it even before his arrival in the city. He remembered the name from when he was held prisoner in the grip of the scarred man's companions in Meung. He had heard that Milady was dangerous. However, he could see no reason to object to her asking a question.

"Go right ahead, Milady."

"Why do you waste your time with those rough musketeers? If you wished it, you could live in the lap of luxury—my lap, to be precise."

D'Artagnan sniffed. "I'll have you know that I'm no one's lap dog, Milady. And I have sworn my loyalty to the king."

"The king!" Milady said with a bitter tone in her voice. "He is weak, and weakness never wins in the end. I advise you to put yourself on the side with those who are strong."

Everybody has advice for me, he thought. *Too bad none of it seems to be good.*

"I am sorry, Milady," D'Artagnan said. "But I prefer to choose my own friends. You may trust my word."

She turned to walk away. D'Artagnan accidentally stepped on the hem of her dress with one paw. The dress immediately slipped from her shoulder. She gasped. At that instant, D'Artagnan saw a *fleur-de-lis* mark on her shoulder. He knew the *fleur-de-lis* was a lily flower sometimes branded onto the flesh of criminals who were scheduled to be executed!

Milady quickly grabbed the cloth and pulled it up to cover the brand. "You will regret your misstep for a long time," she said coldly.

D'Artagnan looked at her. It was impossible not to admire her extraordinary beauty, even though it concealed great evil underneath. She was a dangerous woman to know—and even more frightening when she was made angry.

"Whoa! Sorry," D'Artagnan said. "I can see why you'd like to keep covered up."

"Forget what you have seen. We can still be friends."

"I'm afraid not. Though I try to be a friend to all those who need me, somehow you don't seem as if you'd make a good friend."

D'Artagnan ran down the long hallway, leaving Milady standing there watching him depart.

"No offense," he called back, his words echoing off the walls. He wondered why Milady had once been marked to be executed.

Milady stared after D'Artagnan, an icy smile frozen on her lovely face.

"No offense?" she repeated in a whisper, not intending for D'Artagnan to hear her. "Milady never takes offense. No, indeed. Instead, I take revenge—as you, D'Artagnan, will discover, to your great sorrow. From this moment, you are as good as dead."

On his way back to the barracks where the musketeers trained, D'Artagnan thought about all the things that had happened to him that morning.

First, he had met with and accidentally offended

Cardinal Richelieu. He was the most powerful man in France, not counting the king. The cardinal might have been the most powerful man in France even if you *did* count the king. He would most certainly be a dangerous enemy.

And then D'Artagnan had encountered Milady. D'Artagnan had heard many stories about her. Everyone said that she was a frightful opponent when insulted by one who did not meet with her wishes. It was not in D'Artagnan's nature to give in to others, and Milady's threat had been serious, indeed. Marked as she was with the *fleur-de-lis,* she might very well attempt to cause his death.

Despite his dangerous situation, D'Artagnan was not frightened. On the contrary, he was quite happy. The sun was shining, the ground was warm beneath his paws, and the smells of the city tickled his nose. He had a brave heart, and he had something even more important—true friends.

All for one, and one for all! he thought, as he ambled toward the courtyard of the large public hall of Tréville. He rang the bell, waited, then entered through the courtyard gate to look for his friends, Athos, Porthos, and Aramis.

D'Artagnan was no stranger in the courtyard where the king's guards trained, although he had not yet become a musketeer. Ever since the duel with the cardinal's guardsmen, everyone at the musketeer training school liked him. As for Athos, Porthos, and Aramis, they were constantly in D'Artagnan's company, whether involved in business or pleasure. They saw one another several times a day.

Today, D'Artagnan found his friends in the courtyard. They sat at a table, drinking wine and eating

thick slices of bread. For a moment he stood silently nearby, watching and listening to them.

Athos, as was often the case, looked as if he had something on his mind, some secret sorrow.

Porthos, on the other hand, was quite cheerfully entertaining the other two musketeers with a description of the new cloak he would soon purchase. "It has a red lining," he said. "And it's all black on the outside. I'll look quite dashing in it, don't you think?"

"Oh, no doubt you will," Aramis answered. "And the women will much admire you."

"But not as much as they admire you," Porthos said to Aramis.

"Ah, *mon ami*, I don't know anything about women," Aramis protested.

D'Artagnan's ears perked up as he remembered

the handkerchief that Aramis had covered with his heavy boot.

Athos did not join in the conversation. Instead, he glanced over and noticed D'Artagnan.

"Welcome," he said. "From the look on your face, I would say you have something urgent and unsettling to discuss with us."

Aramis was instantly concerned. "Is something wrong, D'Artagnan?" he asked.

D'Artagnan nodded. "I have good news and bad news."

"Tell us the good news first," Aramis suggested.

"Very well. Today I met Cardinal Richelieu and Milady."

"Very good," Porthos said. "Now, what is the bad news?"

"They dislike me tremendously."

"Ah," Aramis said. "Bad news, indeed."

"They are known to be quite vengeful when they feel that they have been wronged," Athos warned. "And that is not all. The cardinal and Milady are great rivals of the king and queen, to whom we musketeers have pledged our loyalty. You must be very careful, my friend."

"We will be on guard for you," Aramis added. "Your enemies are our enemies."

"All for one, and one for all!" Porthos said.

The musketeers' brave words filled D'Artagnan with pride in his friends. "I knew that you would be supportive of me."

"How will you deal with them?" Aramis asked.

"I'll see what I can sniff out," D'Artagnan said.

D'Artagnan looked at the loaf of bread from which his companions had been eating. He jumped up on a bench next to the table and licked his chops. Then he took a healthy chomp from the loaf.

"I'm hungry. Does anyone care to join me?" he asked.

The others joined D'Artagnan, and the four friends shared the food.

Chapter Nine

*T*he afternoon sunshine came through the school windows, and dust motes floated in the beams of light. Wishbone continued to work his way down the row of lockers, sniffing at each one to see if Mort had dropped down to hide there.

When he came to another slightly open locker door, he pawed it open all the way and looked inside.

Something was moving back there!

Wishbone thought that he certainly had found his rat this time.

"This is it, Mort. You'd better give up before I have to get tough with you."

No response came from within the locker.

"So, silence is your game," he whispered. "Well, no one plays that game better than . . . Stealth Dog."

Wishbone poked his head into the locker and nosed around a bit. He found a blue spiral notebook, a couple of heavy school books, and a gray-cotton jacket hanging from a hook.

Mort was nowhere to be found, but Wishbone was not discouraged.

"Stealth Dog uses the art of disguise!" he said.

Wishbone wiggled himself into the folds of the gray jacket. Soon only his face was sticking out.

"Stealth Dog knows the value of concealment. So which way did Mort go? I'm on his turf, and he's a clever opponent. I'll have to think the way he does. So think . . . rat-like."

Wishbone slipped out from inside the jacket and backed out of the locker. He looked up and down the hallway.

"Nice clean place they have here. But it would be improved by having a dog around."

Wishbone trotted farther down the hallway until he came to the open door of the science lab. There was no one around, so Wishbone went right inside.

"There's the computer, but there's no power cord. That means this is where it all started, with Mort's sharp little teeth. If I just put my nose to work, I'm sure to find some clues to Mort's whereabouts in here."

Wishbone sniffed his way across the floor. Looking up, he saw a plastic skeleton hanging from a hook.

"Helllooo! What's this? A walking X ray?" Wishbone looked around, but there was no sign of the rat. He turned to the skeleton again and said, "Considering the lack of things to eat around here, I can see how you got the way you are. I don't suppose you've seen a white rat sneaking around, have you?"

The skeleton didn't answer.

"Oh, well . . . if you do see him, just be sure to give a yell," Wishbone said.

Wishbone left the skeleton and wandered around the room, sniffing at the feet of the lab tables. There were some very strange smells in the air, aromas that Wishbone couldn't identify.

"It's probably from all the chemicals the kids use in their experiments. If they'd let me hang around in here, I could find out for sure."

Wishbone continued to sniff, and his nose detected another scent. This time, it definitely wasn't chemical.

"Wait a minute! Now I can smell something else. Something ratty. Something that must be . . . Mort!"

Wishbone walked as quietly as he could to the end of one of the lab tables.

"I know he's around here somewhere, and he's close. He won't hear me coming, though. I'm as silent as a panther. As quick as a fox. As brave as a grizzly bear. I have nerves of steel. Nothing can frighten me— not a lion, not a tiger, and certainly not a . . ."

As he was thinking of the things that couldn't frighten him, Wishbone turned the corner of the lab table and found himself face to face with—

"—A RAT! *GAHHhhhhhh!* Rat! Rat! Big! Hairy! Rat!"

Wishbone's sudden appearance startled Mort. He scurried away as fast as his short little legs could carry him. With a twitch of his whiskers, Mort was gone, disappearing behind another table in the lab.

Wishbone skittered backward and found himself beneath a chair.

"I'm not afraid, mind you. I was just a little surprised, that's all. But did you see the face on that thing? *Br-r-r-r-r!* It was enough to give even the bravest dog on earth a little shiver."

There I was, face to face with my enemy, and I had to deal with him. It was just like the way D'Artagnan had to deal with Cardinal Richelieu and Milady.

Chapter Ten

D'Artagnan was certainly concerned about the cardinal and Milady. But soon he had other, more immediate problems to occupy his thoughts.

One evening he was trotting toward the room where he lived. He always enjoyed the smell of the river Seine in the distance, and the aromas of food being served to late diners at restaurants he passed. Suddenly, he heard the loud screams of a young woman echoing from an alleyway.

Running toward the noise, D'Artagnan saw that the woman had been set upon by three men who were pulling at her arms. She seemed in great danger, and D'Artagnan drew his sword at once.

"Step away from her!" D'Artagnan snapped. "Here's someone who can fight back!"

One man remained with the woman, and two of them ran to attack D'Artagnan.

"Two against one?" D'Artagnan said. "Those are the odds I like! Take me if you can!"

One of the men accepted the invitation. He lunged forward with his sword pointed straight at

D'Artagnan's chest. D'Artagnan leaped aside and struck the man with a ringing blow in the side of the head with the pommel of his sword. The man slumped down heavily, clutching his head with both of his hands.

D'Artagnan then turned to deal with the second fellow, who was more cautious.

"Do you think you are a better fighter than I?" D'Artagnan said. "We shall see!"

It was difficult to maneuver in the close quarters of the narrow alley. Suddenly, D'Artagnan spotted a wooden rain barrel nearby. He jumped atop the barrel, balancing on the rim with three legs.

His opponent tried to cut his feet from beneath him. D'Artagnan was able to hop up and allow the sharp blade to whiz by harmlessly beneath him. When his hind feet touched the rim of the barrel again, he stuck the tip of his sword into the man's hat.

"Next I will give you a haircut!" D'Artagnan said with a laugh.

The man did not reply. Instead, he aimed a sharp kick at the barrel. He hoped to knock it out from underneath D'Artagnan. The barrel sailed several feet away, but D'Artagnan was no longer standing on it. He jumped up and over his opponent. He landed easily on the ground and jabbed the man lightly in the back with his sword point.

"Here I am, fellow. Turn around and fight."

His opponent turned, enraged. D'Artagnan stuck his sword into the man's side. The man fell heavily to the ground.

D'Artagnan turned to see that the woman was still struggling with the man who held her as he attempted to drag her away.

"Leave her be, you villain!" D'Artagnan cried. He sprang forward as hard as he could, pushing off with his hind legs.

The man saw that he had to draw his sword and fight. To do so, however, he was forced to release the woman first. So he threw her at D'Artagnan in order to distract him.

D'Artagnan quickly leaped out of the way so the woman would not trip over him. As she found her balance, he turned to her and said, "I beg your pardon, but I have more pressing business at the moment."

He bounced forward toward the man. Light from a candle in a high window fell on the man's face at that instant. D'Artagnan recognized him immediately. It was the man with the ugly scar!

"So we meet again," D'Artagnan said. "I was sure that this moment would come!"

Instantly, the two drew their swords, and blades clattered and clashed together. D'Artagnan quickly gained the advantage in the heated duel. He had done the same during their first fight, at the inn in Meung.

The scarred man devoted every bit of his energy to the fight. His all-out effort was not enough, however. So he resorted to a very underhanded trick. He turned from D'Artagnan and threw his sword like a spear, straight at the young woman.

D'Artagnan, quick as a striking snake, jumped up and caught the sword in his mouth before it could reach its target. He spat it out onto the cobblestones. When he turned back to face his opponent, the man had fled. His two companions got to their feet and quickly followed. The wounded man was helped along by his partner.

"Run, then," D'Artagnan called after them. He turned to the young woman.

"I thank you for your aid," she said gratefully.

D'Artagnan was impressed by the young woman's great physical beauty. It seemed to give some signal of an inner beauty, as well.

"I am called D'Artagnan," he told her. "And what is your name?"

"Constance," she told him. "My full name is Constance Bonacieux."

"Why were those men attacking you?"

"I am the seamstress for the queen. Those men are the cardinal's spies. They believed that I was on a secret mission for Her Majesty. They hoped to force the story from me."

"And *were* you on a mission for the queen?" said D'Artagnan.

"I beg your pardon, but I cannot say, even though you have saved me. Now I must be on my way." With those final words, she ran from the alley, leaving D'Artagnan alone.

I know it's wrong to spy on her, but what if those men of the cardinal haven't given up? I'd better follow her, D'Artagnan thought.

D'Artagnan stayed low to the ground and kept to the deep shadows so he would not be seen. He followed Constance down the street. After going several blocks, she encountered another group of men. D'Artagnan drew his sword.

"Do not touch her, you rogues!" he cried.

The men turned to face him, and their weapons flew into readiness.

"Stop!" Constance said, raising her hands. "There is no need for fighting. D'Artagnan, put away your sword. These men are friends of my mistress, Her Majesty the Queen."

D'Artagnan went forward, his whiskers twitching alertly. He did not sheathe his sword. "Who are they?" he asked.

One of the men stepped forward. "I am the prime minister of England, duke of Buckingham," he announced.

D'Artagnan put away his sword. "I see. I am sorry to have challenged you."

"It is quite all right," the duke said. "You had in mind the protection of a lady."

"True," Constance said. "But now we must be on our way, or you will be late for your meeting. Come with me."

The duke and his men followed Constance to a small house that was set back from the street. D'Artagnan went along with the group. Inside the house, everyone except Buckingham stayed in the entry hall so they would not intrude on the duke's privacy. The duke went into another room and then closed the door.

"Who is he meeting?" D'Artagnan asked.

"The queen," Constance whispered. "They are in love, but it can never be. He asks only that she give him a remembrance of her to take back to England with him."

D'Artagnan understood immediately. If anyone found out that the queen of France and the duke of Buckingham were in love, there would be a great war between England and France.

D'Artagnan's next meeting with Constance did not begin happily. Only two days later she came to his room, weeping.

"What is the matter?" D'Artagnan asked.

"There is great danger for the queen," Constance told him. "There is great peril for all of France, as well. I have been entrusted to find someone to carry a letter to the duke of Buckingham in England. There is no one on whom I can rely."

You can rely on the bravest swordsman in Paris, D'Artagnan thought. He put his paw on Constance's knee. "I hesitate to be so forward, but you are incorrect. There is one individual under this simple thatched roof who would be glad to be of service to you—if you would allow it."

Constance dried her eyes. "If you are speaking of yourself, accept my gratitude. You are my only hope. This letter must be taken to London and put into the hands of the duke of Buckingham. It is from the queen herself."

Constance then went on to explain that the queen had given Buckingham twelve diamond studs as a remembrance.

"Those diamonds were a gift to the queen from the king. The cardinal's spies discovered that the jewels are now in the possession of the duke. The cardinal has suggested that the king ask the queen to wear those very diamonds at a grand ball to be held in twelve days. If she does not wear them, the king will be highly insulted. The duke *must* receive this letter and return the diamonds to the queen in time for the ball."

"And if he does not?" D'Artagnan asked.

Constance looked into his eyes. "If he does not, there will be war between France and England."

The situation was more serious than D'Artagnan had thought, but that did not discourage him. Indeed, it increased his determination to aid both Constance and the queen. In doing so, he would also be helping the entire kingdom of France.

"I will put the letter into the duke's hand myself," D'Artagnan promised.

"It is no small mission that you are about to undertake," Constance told D'Artagnan. "You have only twelve days to travel all the way to England and then to return to France with the diamonds. The cardinal's men will attempt to stop you at every step of the way."

D'Artagnan was not alarmed. "You can rely on me. I have friends who will be glad to assist me."

"Then go now and find them immediately," Constance said. "There must be no delay."

Assuring the young woman that he would make haste, D'Artagnan took his leave.

D'Artagnan went to find Athos, who was in his apartment. By a stroke of good fortune, D'Artagnan found Porthos and Aramis there, as well. He told them that he was going to England on an important mission. "I hope that you will go with me," he added when he was finished.

"But what is the purpose of this mission?" Athos asked.

"I am not at liberty to say. I can only tell you that I have to deliver a most important letter. You will have to trust me when I say that the fate of France hangs in the balance."

"Trust you?" Athos said. "But of course. And if you need my help, I will gladly follow you."

"And I, too," Porthos said.

"And I," Aramis added. "But we must have a plan of action. Where shall we go first?"

D'Artagnan had anticipated the question. "To Calais, on the coast, which is the shortest route from France to England. There is one small problem. I'm afraid that the cardinal may suspect what we are up to. It would please him for us to fail."

"If so," Athos said, "Cardinal Richelieu will stop at nothing, even murder, to prevent you from reaching your destination."

Murder? D'Artagnan thought. His whiskers began to twitch. *I don't think so.*

D'Artagnan did not hesitate. "If I am killed, then one of you will have to take the letter. No matter what happens to me, or to any of us, the letter *must* reach the duke of Buckingham in London!"

It was two o'clock in the morning when they finished their discussion. D'Artagnan and the musketeers rode immediately out of Paris. The houses were all quiet, and scarcely a candle burned in all of the city. The moon threw long shadows on the cobbled streets. The hooves of the foursome's horses echoed eerily off the stone walls that lined the narrow streets. No one spoke a word as the companions began the first leg of their long and dangerous journey.

Chapter Eleven

D'Artagnan was pleasantly surprised when he and his partners encountered no problems during the first stage of their journey. No highwaymen sprang out of the woods to ambush or rob them. No members of the cardinal's guard stopped them and demanded that they return to Paris. Everything went exactly as planned.

Maybe the cardinal can't be bothered with chasing after a mere letter, D'Artagnan mused.

He and his friends had stopped for breakfast at an inn in Chantilly, ninety miles north of Paris. The atmosphere was friendly, and the air was full of the tempting aromas of ham and eggs and warm bread.

D'Artagnan hopped up onto a seat and prepared to order one of everything on the menu. He noted that the mood in the dining room of the inn was cheerful and carefree.

That changed for the worse when a stranger entered the room. The man ordered wine. When he had received his drink, he said to Porthos, who was standing near him, "Here's to the health of Cardinal Richelieu. Drink with me!"

Porthos tried to be pleasant. "Gladly," he said. "But only if you will agree to drink with me to the health of the king."

The stranger set his wineglass down carefully on the table. One hand was hovering near his sword. "You will drink to the cardinal, or you will die," he said.

"You are making a serious mistake, my friend," Porthos replied.

The stranger frowned. "I am *not* your friend."

"No," Porthos agreed. "You are not. And you're never likely to be, not after I've poked you full of holes. *En garde!*"

Both men whipped out their swords from their sheaths. The blades clashed together like a pair of giant cymbals. The inn was filled with the sounds of clanging steel. D'Artagnan and the other musketeers moved away from the intense action as Porthos forced the stranger backward. A table was overturned; wine spilled from the stranger's glass and splashed all over the floor.

"You fiend!" the stranger yelled.

The dueling grew more furious. D'Artagnan looked at his three companions as if to ask them what to do.

It was Athos who spoke. "This is some trick of the cardinal's," he said. "This stranger was sent here to kill you, and Porthos has distracted him. We must leave here at once."

D'Artagnan called across the room to Porthos, "We must leave you here to finish what you have begun. Make short work of the fellow. Then join us as soon as you can."

"I will carve up this piece of mutton!" Porthos said. "Be on your way."

D'Artagnan hopped from his chair, landing gently on his front paws, and started for the door.

He turned back to see Porthos still fencing with his foe. D'Artagnan thought he saw a smile on his friend's face and realized that Porthos was enjoying himself.

He'll be fine, D'Artagnan thought. His spirits lifted as he reminded himself that Porthos could take care of himself in any situation. His tail wagged as he headed out the door.

In the courtyard, D'Artagnan, Athos, and Aramis leaped into their saddles and rode away. But soon enough they found themselves in trouble again.

About a mile beyond the village of Beauvais, northwest of Chantilly, the road passed between two high embankments. There were a number of men there, eight to be exact. They seemed to be filling the holes in the road with hard-packed mud.

I don't like the smell of this, D'Artagnan thought, his nose twitching.

As the musketeers and D'Artagnan passed by, the workers began jeering and sneering at them.

"Here, now," one of them said. "Don't disturb our work. We can't have travelers messing up the road while we're trying to repair it."

"And I cannot have mud soiling my fine boots," Aramis said. "Move out of our way, and let us pass."

"We will let no man pass without receiving our permission," the worker said. "And you do not have it. Now, men! Take them!"

The "crew" of road repairers were not really laborers at all. They ran to a ditch beside the road and jumped in. When they came into view again, they were all armed with muskets. They opened fire on the travelers. Puffs of smoke billowed into the sky, the sound of shots exploded in the air, and musket balls whizzed by D'Artagnan and the musketeers.

Aramis cried out and fell from his horse. Blood poured from a shoulder wound.

D'Artagnan was the first to realize what was happening. "It's an ambush! Don't try to charge them! Ride forward!"

Aramis, although he was wounded, grasped the mane of his horse, lifted his legs, and let the animal carry him forward with the others. Even with his shoulder wound, he was able to pull himself into the saddle and ride.

The firing continued. A musket ball tore D'Artagnan's hat from his head. He flattened his ears down. "I'd better lie low. I almost became a headless horseman! These are the cardinal's men!" D'Artagnan shouted. "This attack is just another attempt by the cardinal to prevent us from reaching our destination. Let us be gone!"

They rode swiftly away to safety. Aramis was so severely wounded that his companions had to leave him at an inn in Crèvecœur, where his injury could be cared for properly.

When Athos and D'Artagnan had left their friend, Athos said, "Now there are only two of us to make sure that the letter reaches its destination. I hope that we do not fail in our mission."

They stayed for the night at a travelers' lodge in the town of Amiens, thirty miles north of Beauvais. They arrived at midnight, tired and ready for rest.

The next day, when they checked on their horses,

Athos said to D'Artagnan, "Our horses are exhausted. Maybe you could sniff around the neighborhood and see if anyone has two good horses for sale. I'll settle the bill here at the inn."

D'Artagnan agreed, but he was suspicious of his surroundings. *I wonder if this is another trick that involves a little birdie—a red bird, like a cardinal*, he thought.

D'Artagnan's doubts caused him to hang back when Athos went inside to pay their bill. Instead of going to look for horses to buy, D'Artagnan stood just outside the lodge's door to watch for trouble.

Athos found the innkeeper. He was sitting in a little room that served him as an office. The man was seated behind his desk, taking care of his bookkeeping chores.

Athos took out two coins and gave them to the man, saying, "My friend and I will be leaving now. Here is the money for our night's lodging."

The innkeeper smiled, and Athos put the money into his hand. As soon as the money touched his palm, the man's smile vanished. He looked very closely at the coins and turned them over and over in his hands. Then with a shout, he threw the coins across the room. They bounced off the wall and then rolled across the floor and under the desk.

"This money is counterfeit!" the innkeeper yelled. "I will have you arrested at once!"

Athos, inflamed by the man's accusation, drew out his sword immediately.

"You insulting scoundrel!" he said.

D'Artagnan had heard the heated argument between the two men. He started to go inside to prevent his friend from getting into further trouble, but he was too late. As he stepped across the threshold, four men

78

entered the innkeeper's office through side doors. All four of the men were armed to the teeth, and all four of them were intent on capturing Athos . . . or killing him.

"It is another trap!" Athos shouted at the top of his lungs. "They have succeeded in tricking us again! Flee, D'Artagnan!"

Fleas? Where are they? I hate *fleas! . . . Oh, wait a minute. He said* "flee."

"Make haste!" Athos cried. "You must go on and ride swiftly!"

D'Artagnan hated the idea of leaving Athos, but he knew Athos was right. Somehow, D'Artagnan had to succeed in his mission. The honor of his queen and the fate of his country were at stake.

That thought put extra energy into his step and he raced, pushing his four paws to the limit. He ran to the hitching rail and untied one of the horses with his teeth. Then he leaped up onto the rail itself and then onto the horse. Hanging on for dear life, he rode like the wind.

"Brave Athos," D'Artagnan said to himself. "But the same thing may happen to me at any time. And yet it must not. The letter *must* get through to the duke of Buckingham!"

He turned the horse toward the coastal city of Calais and galloped away.

Wow! The attacks launched by the cardinal's guards are really coming at a fast and furious pace. Speaking of attacks, let's sniff on over to the science lab and see if I can finally spring a trap to catch the rat. . . .

Chapter Twelve

Wishbone sniffed along the floor of the science lab. He tried to relocate Mort, who was no longer anywhere to be seen.

"Doggone it! I've lost the scent. Where is that cord-chewing rat, anyway? He could be lurking around here anywhere, or he could be gone already."

Wishbone started walking toward the skeleton. He came to a stop when he heard a noise coming from somewhere above him. He looked up and saw a glass lab beaker being nudged toward the edge of the lab table where he was standing.

"A glass beaker moving across the table all by itself? Now, there's something you don't see every day. If what I know about gravity is true, then any minute now that glass—"

Wishbone darted away from the table just in time. The beaker, having extended more than halfway over the edge, came crashing to the floor. It shattered into slivers right on the very spot where Wishbone had been standing only micro-seconds before. Wishbone got splashed with water . . . or what he hoped was only water. He didn't want his shiny coat to suddenly start dissolving.

"A vicious, sneak attack! Just what you'd expect from a rat! But Stealth Dog is too quick for him."

Wishbone sniffed the puddle of liquid, carefully avoiding the glass splinters that lay all over the floor. It was water, all right.

Wishbone looked up at the tabletop to see what had caused the beaker to fall. He spotted Mort's twitchy little nose poking over the edge and sniffing the air. Then Wishbone saw the rat's beady black eyes. Mort peered down, as if to see whether the beaker had made contact with its target.

"That's right, rat," Wishbone said. "You missed. You're in *big* trouble now. Now it's personal!"

At Wishbone's words, Mort fled. He stretched his white body to its full length as he scampered from tabletop to tabletop. Wishbone followed along, but his route of pursuit took him under the tables.

"You take the high road, Mort, and I'll take the low road," Wishbone said. "But Stealth Dog will be in the computer lab before you."

Wishbone heard the rat bounce off a test-tube holder and rattle against a Bunsen burner.

"Watch your step, rat. I wouldn't want anything to happen to you before I get you."

Mort made no reply. Wishbone heard him fall into a sink. He heard the scratching of tiny claws scrabbling against the slippery side as Mort struggled to climb out.

Wishbone jumped up on a nearby chair. Before he could make the big leap over to the sink, Mort had scrambled out and was on his way again.

The door! Wishbone thought.

Wishbone put on a burst of speed, but Mort had a head start. He bounced into the air, landed with all four feet churning, and sped through the doorway like a white blur before Wishbone could get there.

Wishbone put on the brakes and skidded to a stop just short of the lab doorway. Then he poked his head out and looked up and down the hallway.

All he saw was lockers and walls. No Mort. Not a sign or a smell.

Wishbone heard another noise come from somewhere down the hall. Mort was into more mischief.

Wishbone charged out the door. A third noise reached his ears as he ran down the hallway. That Mort was a regular one-rat wrecking crew . . . but not for much longer.

"Ready or not, Mort," Wishbone barked, "here I come."

Chapter Thirteen

D'Artagnan's horse stopped a hundred yards from the seaport of Calais. Leaving the horse beside the road, D'Artagnan trotted toward the town. It did not take him long to sniff out the dock area. He could smell tar and fish and salty water somewhere to the north, and he went in that direction.

Arriving at the dock, he saw a tall sailing ship that was being loaded, probably to cross the English Channel to England. The boat rocked gently on the swell of the water, and the lines that held it fast to the dock creaked with the strain.

White gulls wheeled in the blue sky above the ship, swooping and diving toward the water, which was almost as blue as the sky.

Near the ship stood a gentleman who appeared to be in as great a hurry as D'Artagnan. He was talking to the ship's captain, and he had a distinctive scar on his face.

Ah-ha! thought D'Artagnan. *So we meet for the third time. Strike one. Strike two. Third time, you are out!*

D'Artagnan quickly ducked for cover. He stuck his

nose out from between some cargo barrels to watch and listen without being seen.

"You should have come yesterday," the captain was saying to the man. "An order has arrived from Cardinal Richelieu. We are now forbidden to transport passengers to England without the personal permission of His Eminence."

"The cardinal strikes yet again!" whispered D'Artagnan. "This guy is really starting to get on my nerves."

The man with the scar took a paper from his pocket and said, "I have the cardinal's permission. Here it is."

The ship's master hardly glanced at the paper. "You'll have to show that to the governor of the port. He's spending the day at his country house."

The gentleman did not like that news. "And where is this country house located?"

"In the country, I'll bet," said D'Artagnan in a whisper.

"In the country, of course," the captain told the scar-faced man. "But it isn't far away. Look," he said, pointing. "You can see it from here."

The scarred fellow turned on his heel and left the dock. D'Artagnan waited until he had gone several paces and then decided to tail him.

Once outside the city, they entered a wooded area. It was then that D'Artagnan overtook the man.

"I beg your pardon, *monsieur*," D'Artagnan said. "You seem to be in quite a hurry. Nevertheless, I must ask you a favor."

"And what is that?" the scar-faced man asked, looking warily at D'Artagnan.

"Allow me to sail first."

The gentleman shook his head. "That's impossible. I was here first, and I shall sail first."

"Not true," D'Artagnan said. "I will sail before you. There is one other little matter, too. I must have that letter of permission you are carrying, since I do not have one of my own."

The man peered closely at him. "Why, I recognize you! You're the country bumpkin again from the inn at Meung! You have caused me a great deal of trouble in the past. I will not allow you to take my letter."

"Nevertheless, I must have it."

"Try, then!" the man cried, drawing his sword. "But you will not have it!"

Almost before the fight had begun, D'Artagnan had wounded his adversary three times. After the third sword thrust, the man fell heavily to his knees. Then he toppled over right on his nose.

You won't be working with the cardinal against the king anymore today, D'Artagnan thought, *and not for a few days more, at least.*

D'Artagnan kneeled down next to the man and stuck his mouth into his coat pocket to retrieve the letter. As soon as D'Artagnan had bent down, the man, who had not dropped his sword, suddenly leaped up and struck D'Artagnan in the chest with his weapon.

So, he was only playing dead! The oldest trick in the book! D'Artagnan silently scolded himself for being conned.

The man cried out, "And here's one for you!"

D'Artagnan felt the sting of the man's sword, as it parted the fur on his shoulder and cut into his sensitive hide.

"And here's one from me!" D'Artagnan answered.

He wounded the man for the fourth time. The man fell yet again. This time he did not move as D'Artagnan searched his clothing for the letter. He found it in a pocket and pulled it out with his teeth. He looked at it and saw that it was made out in the name of the Comte de Wardes.

D'Artagnan licked his wound. Luckily, it was neither painful nor serious. Then he walked to the country house of the port's governor.

The servant at the country house announced him to the governor as "the Comte." D'Artagnan explained that he wished to travel to London.

"Is your mission truly of the utmost urgency?" the governor asked.

"Oh, absolutely. I have a letter signed by the cardinal himself," he added, offering the governor the letter in his mouth.

"It seems to be perfectly in order," the governor said after a moment's examination. "You must have this letter if you want to sail, because the cardinal is trying to prevent some scoundrel from traveling to London. His name is D'Artagnan."

"I know him very well," D'Artagnan said. *Almost as well as I know myself*, he thought.

"Describe him, then."

"He's quite a brave young man, I must say," D'Artagnan began.

He proceeded to describe the man he had left lying wounded in the woods.

"Look for the scar," D'Artagnan said. "You can't miss the scar."

"We will keep a sharp lookout for him," the governor said.

An excellent idea. Too bad I won't be around to see the look on his face when you arrest him, thought D'Artagnan with amusement.

"I'll be sure to tell the cardinal of your vigilance when I see him," D'Artagnan said.

The governor was pleased. "Thank you. And please tell him that I am his humble servant."

"Of course," D'Artagnan said.

The governor countersigned the letter and then returned it to him.

With the letter held firmly in his teeth, D'Artagnan made his way back to the dock, where the ship was almost fully loaded. He gave his letter to the captain.

"Everything is in order," the captain said. Then he handed back the letter. "But now you must get on board, for we will be sailing within the half hour."

D'Artagnan was on board in five minutes. He waited impatiently for the hoisting of the sails. Soon the anchor was weighed, and the ship moved away from the dock. They had not been sailing for more than ten minutes when D'Artagnan heard the sound of a cannon being fired.

"What does that mean?" he asked the captain.

"It means the port has been closed," the captain answered. "No more ships will be allowed to sail from the port. You are fortunate to have gotten on this boat when you did."

Just call me a lucky dog, D'Artagnan thought. He lay down on the deck, rested his head on his paws, and took a well-deserved nap.

Chapter Fourteen

Wishbone entered another classroom and scanned the entire room quickly. Then he jumped up on the teacher's desk and took a position behind a flowerpot that was filled with bright yellow chrysanthemums.

"Stealth Dog recognizes the advantages of having a good lookout point," he said.

Wishbone scanned the classroom again, looking for signs of Mort. The rat had entered the room earlier. Wishbone could smell him. But he couldn't see him.

He saw the students' desks, arranged in rows, and the pictures of famous Americans on the bulletin board. He smelled chalk and flowers. He smelled meat loaf again, too.

"Boy, that meat loaf odor sure lingers. I wonder if it's as good as Ellen's."

Wishbone licked his chops as he thought about the heavenly taste of meat loaf.

"Wait just a minute here. I can't start thinking about food—not while I'm on a stake-out."

There was a noise in the hall. Wishbone hunkered down behind the flowerpot.

"That sounds a little too big to be Mort. But maybe he got into some weird chemicals in the lab, and now he's fifty feet tall—like one of those rats in the science-fiction movies."

A giant shadow fell across the doorway.

"Uh-oh! He *is* a giant!" Wishbone exclaimed.

Instead of sighting Mort, however, Wishbone saw Mr. Brassfield enter the room.

Wishbone was relieved. "Oh, it's only you. I was expecting somebody else. A giant rat, actually. No offense."

"What are you doing on that desk?" Mr. Brassfield said. "I thought I told you there were no dogs allowed in school."

Wishbone stood up. "I know, and I told you I'd inform any dogs that I saw. But I haven't seen any. I've seen a rat, though. A big, scary one. But don't worry. I'll catch him."

When Mr. Brassfield began to make his way directly toward Wishbone, the terrier jumped down from the desk and sprinted for the door.

Sorry I can't stick around, but I have a rat to trap!

Wishbone zipped into the hallway and left Mr. Brassfield behind.

"All right, Mort," Wishbone said. "Come out with your nose twitching and your whiskers and tail up."

Wishbone looked to the right and to the left. He glanced through the doorway of every classroom that he passed.

"Playing hard-to-get, huh, Mort? Well, you can't hide from me forever. Sooner or later I'll find you, even if I have to search the whole building."

Wishbone could hear Mr. Brassfield whistling—whistling for Wishbone to come.

"I hope he doesn't think I'm going to fall for that old gag. I only answer to Joe's whistle. Stealth Dog is on a special assignment."

Joe entered the school carrying the new power cord for the computer. Sam and David followed close behind him. They re-entered the school building just in time to hear Mr. Brassfield whistling.

"What's that noise?" Sam asked.

"It sounds as if someone's whistling," David answered. "It seems to be coming from the second floor."

Joe agreed. "Let's check it out."

They went up the stairs and saw Mr. Brassfield standing in the middle of the hallway.

"Hi, Mr. Brassfield," Joe called. "What's going on?"

"It's that dog of yours," Mr. Brassfield said. "He got into the building somehow. I'm going to have to put him out. No dogs are allowed in school, you know."

Mr. Brassfield turned and walked down the hallway, whistling again. Suddenly, Joe realized that Mr. Brassfield was whistling to attract Wishbone. Now he was worried. He didn't want Wishbone to get into trouble.

"I'd better find Wishbone before Mr. Brassfield does," Joe said.

"I'll help you look for him," Sam suggested.

"I'll help, too," David said. "Let's go find him. That CD-ROM can wait."

"Great," Joe said. "Now, since Mr. Brassfield is going *that* way, we'll go *this* way."

91

Chapter Fifteen

After a long trip on sea and land, D'Artagnan arrived in London. The muddy streets were full of people hurrying here and there. They all seemed to know exactly where they were going, unlike D'Artagnan.

After asking for directions on the street, D'Artagnan found the home of the duke of Buckingham. The house was a magnificent structure, with many towers and balconies. D'Artagnan trotted up a gravel path to the front door. He stretched up on his hind legs and scratched at the door with his front paws.

The knock was answered by the duke's personal valet, who introduced himself as Patrick.

"And what is your business here?" Patrick asked.

"I must see the duke at once," D'Artagnan said. He wagged his tail briskly for emphasis. "I have come all the way from Paris on a mission of life and death."

The urgency in D'Artagnan's voice must have convinced Patrick to allow the young man in to see Buckingham. Patrick announced, "I will take you to him at once."

He led D'Artagnan straight to the duke's private sitting room, where the duke was going over some papers. Buckingham looked up when Patrick entered.

"There is a young Frenchman to see you, sir," Patrick said.

"You look familiar," the duke of Buckingham told D'Artagnan. "Have we met?"

"Yes—in Paris," D'Artagnan replied. "I bring you an urgent message from the queen."

"Has some misfortune befallen the queen?" the duke asked anxiously.

"Not yet," D'Artagnan answered. "But something bad could happen soon—and not only to her. You must read this letter I have brought."

D'Artagnan stood up on his hind legs with the letter in his mouth.

The duke took the letter from him and unfolded it. "What is this hole in the paper?" he asked before he began to read.

"Nothing," D'Artagnan said.

Nothing, that is, if you don't count the fact that someone stuck the point of a sword right through it . . . and into me.

The duke read through the letter, his face mirroring his great concern. His appearance became more and more worried as he went on.

"This is indeed bad news," he said when he had finished reading.

He walked over to one of the room's walls and took a golden key from a chain around his neck. The wall was covered with a heavy curtain, which the duke pushed aside. Behind the curtain was a hidden door that the duke unlocked with the key. In seconds the door swung open.

"Follow me," the duke told D'Artagnan.

They passed through the doorway to enter a small room lighted by many candles and hung with tapestries. On one wall was a portrait of the queen of France. On a table below the portrait was a carved box in which the duke kept the diamond studs.

"The queen gave me these studs to remember her by," the duke said. "I thought I would have them always. But because she needs them so desperately, I will gladly return them to her."

He smiled as he reached to pick them up. However, when his hand had barely touched them, he gave a great cry.

"I've been robbed! There were twelve studs here, but now two of them are missing!"

"And if my math is correct, twelve minus two equals . . . big trouble," D'Artagnan said.

The duke held up the studs to show D'Artagnan.

"See? The ribbon that held them has been cut. Someone has snipped off two of them."

"Who could it have been?" D'Artagnan asked.

"I have no idea," the duke replied. "Wait," the duke said, his brow furrowed in thought. "I wore these studs only once—to a ball that my king gave eight days ago, after I returned from France. There was a woman there—a beautiful French woman who seemed very interested in the gems."

I'm going to give myself three guesses as to who that woman was. And I won't need the last two, D'Artagnan thought.

"Was her name Milady?" D'Artagnan asked.

The duke's face showed his surprise. "It was! How could you possibly know her?"

"She is an agent of Cardinal Richelieu."

"Of course!" the duke said. "I should have suspected that. The cardinal has placed spies all over the world. And this one has ruined us, unless . . . How soon is this ball for which the queen must have the diamonds?"

"It is to be held in five days."

"Then we must hurry. Patrick!" the duke called. Patrick suddenly appeared in the room beside them. "Yes, my lord?" Patrick said.

"Bring my jeweler to me—at once."

Two days later, Patrick escorted D'Artagnan back to the port. D'Artagnan left England in a small boat, continuing his top-secret mission. He hoped to reach the French coast, and then go on to Paris, before it was too late.

Chapter Sixteen

D'Artagnan arrived on horseback at the royal residence after the ball had already begun. Without an invitation, he was turned away at the front gate. From where he stood, he heard the cheers of the crowd inside as the queen entered the great palace ballroom.

"If I don't get to her, the king may find out about her love for the duke of Buckingham and accuse her of treason," D'Artagnan said. He looked around for an unguarded entrance, but he could find none anywhere. "Well . . . it looks as if it's up and over, then," he said to himself.

D'Artagnan backed away from the high palace wall and got a running start. Stretching to his full length, he pushed hard with his hind legs and leaped atop his horse. He hardly touched the saddle before he sprang again, this time to the top of the wall.

"Stop him!" a guard yelled, but D'Artagnan had already disappeared over the wall.

The king entered the ballroom in full royal dress. He looked very much like the leader of his country. It was not long before he saw that the queen was not wearing her diamonds.

Responding to his look, the queen told him, "You know I always keep them locked away, for fear that they might be stolen. However, if you really wish for me to wear them, I can send for them."

"Please do so at once," the king said. "I am eager to see how they look with your gown."

The queen, greatly worried, went to seek Constance and to ask her what to do. She was very afraid that she was going to have to disappoint the king. His dissatisfaction could well be dangerous to her. Not only that, but it could end up meaning war between France and England. Never before had so much depended on twelve missing diamonds and one almost-musketeer!

Once the queen was out of the ballroom, Cardinal Richelieu, who had made sure he was invited to the party, joined the king. "Good evening, Your Majesty," he said.

"Good evening," the king replied. "What is that box you have in your hand?"

The cardinal opened a small wooden box. Inside were two diamond studs that Milady had handed over to the cardinal earlier that evening. Milady had returned from London to Paris around the same time that evening as D'Artagnan had. However, she had not been turned away at the palace gate. She had handed over the studs to the cardinal as soon as she had arrived at the palace.

"Why, those are exactly like the ones I gave the queen," the king said in surprise after he had examined the studs. "What does this mean?"

"Nothing at all," the cardinal said. "But if the

queen is wearing her diamonds, please count them, Your Majesty. If there are only ten, kindly ask Her Majesty who has the other two."

D'Artagnan ran in the shadows of the palace wall. Thick ivy covered the wall. He began to climb the trellis on which the ivy grew.

Cats are better at this sort of thing, D'Artagnan thought. The shouts of the guards added to his sense of urgency. Soon he was crawling inside a window into a room. It was dark, but he could make out a door at the other side of the room. He made his way across the room and pushed the door open with his nose. Then he peered out into a wide hallway.

"Wow! I've finally made it into the palace. Now, if I can only find the queen in time!" he said.

D'Artagnan found Constance weeping in one of the queen's chambers. "If you are crying for me, you can stop now," he said.

"D'Artagnan!" Constance cried. "I knew that if anyone could accomplish this dangerous mission, it would be you."

"I had the help of valiant friends," D'Artagnan said, but Constance did not hear him. She was looking at the diamond studs that he held out to her.

With a cry of joy, she took the diamonds from D'Artagnan. She ran from the room and down the hall, to find the queen. The queen gazed at the studs, thought of Buckingham, and sighed. Then she fastened the gems to her gown with great relief. D'Artagnan knew that the cardinal was responsible for the king's request to have her wear the jewels. Now the cardinal's plans to start trouble would be thwarted.

D'Artagnan followed the queen back to the ballroom and hid himself behind a heavy curtain. He watched the queen re-enter the ballroom. He heard a cry of admiration from every mouth there. Not only was the queen the most beautiful woman in all of France, but the diamonds shone brilliantly in the light from all the flickering candles and torches. The king and the cardinal saw that the queen was wearing the studs, but D'Artagnan knew they could not count them from across the room.

Before there was any opportunity for counting, the dancing began. The king and queen were the first couple to dance. Taking the queen's hand, the king led her through the formal steps. They wove around one

another as the queen twirled gracefully. Each time the king was close to the queen, he attempted to count the diamonds, but each time she would turn exactly at the critical moment and foil his efforts. D'Artagnan knew the king would probably be suspecting that she was trying to hide the fact that two of the diamond studs were missing.

Meanwhile, D'Artagnan could see the cardinal looking on and breaking out in a cold sweat. The cardinal was eager to cause trouble, and D'Artagnan knew that the cardinal thought the queen was wearing only ten diamond studs.

When the dance ended at last, the king took the box from the cardinal and walked over to the queen. "I am glad you have agreed with my wishes and worn the diamonds," the king said. "But I believe you have lost two of them."

He opened the box and showed her its contents. The two studs sparkled against the black-velvet lining.

The queen acted surprised. "Why, sire, how wonderful! You are giving me two more diamonds! Now I shall have fourteen!"

At that, the king counted the diamonds the queen was wearing. To his surprise and puzzlement, there were twelve of them, after all. He turned and called for the cardinal.

"What is the meaning of this?" the king asked when Cardinal Richelieu reached them. "You have given me two diamond studs, but the queen already has the twelve that I gave her. She does not need two more."

D'Artagnan could see the cardinal was furious at having his plot ruined. Under the circumstances, however, there was nothing he could do except try to appear gracious.

"What this means," the cardinal said, hiding his frustration as best he could, "is that I wanted to present Her Majesty with these two diamond studs to match the dozen you had already given her. Not daring to offer them myself, I hoped that she might accept them as coming from you."

The queen smiled at him to let him know that she was wise to his little scheme. "I am grateful to Your Eminence," she said sweetly. "I am sure these studs cost you as much as all twelve of those that the king gave me."

The cardinal ground his teeth in rage, but he did not let the queen see. D'Artagnan, however, grinned happily at the cardinal's frustration.

Later in the evening, Constance met D'Artagnan and led him to a corridor some distance away from the ballroom. She told him to stay behind another heavy curtain that rubbed softly against his fur.

What's this? D'Artagnan thought. *A little game of hide-and-seek?*

D'Artagnan was puzzled, but he did as he was told. Before long, a woman's hand came through an opening in the curtain. The hand was held in a position to be kissed, and D'Artagnan responded gallantly. Then the hand dropped something to the floor. D'Artagnan looked down and saw a golden ring.

Looking up from the ring, he heard footsteps moving rapidly away down the hall. He could not resist taking a peek from behind the curtain.

He saw only a masked woman whom he could not identify. Nevertheless, he was certain that it was the queen. He knew that he would keep the ring always. He would remember forever the service that he had performed for Her Majesty, and the lovely gift that she had given him in return.

Chapter Seventeen

D'Artagnan was pleased with himself and the outcome of his mission. With success in that area, he was now determined to discover the fate of his three companions. He went first to the inn at Chantilly, where Porthos had fought with the stranger.

When he went inside, he said to the innkeeper, "You may remember that some days ago I came here with my friends. One of them was engaged in a duel against another man when I departed."

"Of course, *monsieur,*" the host answered. "It is not something that I could forget. Your friend was . . . I cannot say it." To D'Artagnan, the host looked almost embarrassed. The innkeeper's hesitant manner immediately aroused D'Artagnan's curiosity.

"You may tell me," D'Artagnan said. "I am his friend, and I have only his best interests at heart."

The host looked doubtful, but he gave in. "Monsieur Porthos was seriously wounded. Though he boasted that he would best the stranger, your friend received a severe wound."

And how severe was it? thought D'Artagnan.

The host continued. "Monsieur Porthos stumbled over a chair, and the stranger stuck him in . . . well, his . . . his rump."

D'Artagnan wagged his tail happily. "A severely embarrassing wound, indeed."

"Absolutely. But then the stranger put his sword at Monsieur Porthos's throat, asking him his name. When Porthos told him, the stranger assisted him in rising, saying that he had no further quarrel with him. The stranger was looking for a young swordsman named D'Artagnan."

Just as I suspected. It's the cardinal's dirty doings again. What a sneak that cardinal is! D'Artagnan thought.

"And is Porthos better now?" D'Artagnan asked.

"But of course. I will show you to his room, but you must be careful of your friend. He has threatened to shoot anyone who sticks his head into the room, because we have had the nerve to ask him to pay his bill."

Typical Porthos. Some things never change.

D'Artagnan promised to be careful.

The host took him upstairs to a room where Porthos was lying on his stomach, reading. He gave a shout of joy at seeing his friend, and D'Artagnan asked how his wound was healing.

"It's a mere scratch—nothing serious."

That's exactly what I'd say under the same circumstances, D'Artagnan thought.

"But you are better now?"

"Quite well. And I'm ready to leave."

"I will take care of the bill if you are ready to ride. Does that . . . er . . . *sit* well with you?"

"Of course. Why do you ask?"

"Oh, no reason," D'Artagnan said. Then he told Porthos the entire story of his adventures.

"And you have heard nothing of Athos and Aramis since your return?" Porthos asked when D'Artagnan had finished.

"I have not," D'Artagnan said. "I can only hope that they will be as well as you."

"Let us go and see," Porthos said.

When Porthos and D'Artagnan rode up to the inn at Crèvecœur, where D'Artagnan had last seen Aramis, they were greeted outside by the innkeeper.

"*Bonjour,*" D'Artagnan said. "Can you tell me what has become of a friend of mine whom I left here a number of days ago? He had a musket wound to his shoulder."

"He is still here, *monsieur,*" the innkeeper replied.

D'Artagnan leaped from his saddle to the ground, his tail wagging excitedly. "Your words give me new life! Lead me to my friend so that I might embrace him!"

"But a priest and a monk are with him now."

"Oh, no!" D'Artagnan exclaimed. "Then he must be dying! Take me to him immediately!"

The innkeeper laughed. "Oh, he is not dying, *monsieur.* He is doing very well. The priest is with him because he has decided to devote himself to a life of meditation."

Of course. I should have remembered, D'Artagnan thought. *He told me when we first met that he was going to be a priest. I just didn't think it would happen so soon.*

"Then take me to him, anyway," D'Artagnan said. "I must see him and be able to convince myself that he is all right."

The innkeeper led D'Artagnan inside to a room and opened the door. When D'Artagnan looked in, he saw that Aramis was lying in bed, speaking to two men dressed all in black.

"D'Artagnan!" Aramis said when he saw his friend. "I had almost given up hope of seeing you again."

"And I had not thought to see you, either," D'Artagnan responded. "I feared that your wound had killed you. But I see that it has not. I am glad to see that you are alive. I will not stay, however. I believe that you must be giving your confession to these men."

"No," Aramis said. "I am talking to them about devoting my life to meditation and prayer."

"I understand," D'Artagnan said. "I suppose that means you will not want to help me find Athos, who may be dead or wounded. And I assume that you do not ever want to fight at my side again. Ah, well, a life of quiet solitude is good for some men, while others prefer a life of action and adventure."

Aramis looked thoughtful.

"And of course there is Porthos," D'Artagnan said. "But I suppose you wouldn't want to see him. He would only remind you of all the good times you and he had together, matching swords with the cardinal's men."

Aramis threw back the bedcovers and jumped from the bed.

"It is time for me to leave," Aramis said to the priests as they left the room. "I am not yet ready for the quiet life. I must help my friends."

Aramis dressed quickly, put on his sword, and turned to D'Artagnan.

"You say that Athos is in trouble?"

"We will go and find out," D'Artagnan said. "Pray that Athos will be waiting for us."

"I've prayed that already," Aramis said.

Together, Aramis, Porthos, and D'Artagnan rode to Amiens. When they arrived, Aramis and Porthos stayed with the horses. D'Artagnan walked boldly into the inn and demanded to speak to the innkeeper. This was the same innkeeper who had once threatened to have Athos arrested.

When D'Artagnan saw the man, he growled, showed his teeth, and snapped, "I have come for my friend Athos. When I last saw him, he was battling four men. What have you done with him?"

"Please, *monsieur*," the frightened innkeeper said. "Do not be angry. Only wait a moment and listen to my story."

D'Artagnan realized that he had let his temper get the best of him. He tried to put a leash on his anger.

"I will tell you everything, *monsieur*," the innkeeper said. "You see, I had been warned by the authorities that some counterfeiters were traveling this way. I was given descriptions that matched you and your friend exactly."

Three guesses as to which authority sent out that information—and I don't need the last two guesses, thought D'Artagnan.

"Who gave you these descriptions?" D'Artagnan asked.

"A man representing Cardinal Richelieu," the

innkeeper answered. "I knew only that I was to help catch the counterfeiters. I just did my part."

"Very well. And what happened after I was gone?"

"Your friend defended himself desperately. He shot two men, wounded one man with his sword, and stunned me by hitting me in the head with the flat side of his weapon."

"But where is he now?"

"During the fighting, your friend found the key to my storage cellar. He unlocked the door, went inside, and barricaded himself behind it. He remains there even now. He will not let me down there to get to any of my supplies."

D'Artagnan wagged his tail and laughed.

"It is not a laughing matter, *monsieur,*" the innkeeper complained. "When I last tried to go into the cellar, I could hear him loading his muskets."

The innkeeper showed D'Artagnan the door to the cellar. D'Artagnan called out to his friend, telling him that all was well.

"Thank goodness you have come, D'Artagnan," Athos said as he finally emerged from the cellar. "I was tired of that dank hole. There was nothing but bad wine to drink and stale sausages to eat."

"Oh, my wine!" the innkeeper exclaimed, running to the cellar. Soon there was a loud howl from inside. The innkeeper had discovered something else. "The villain has gnawed all my sausages!"

"It was probably rats. Cellars sometimes have rats," said D'Artagnan with a wag of his tail.

"And there are many broken bottles! Wine is flooding all over the floor," complained the innkeeper.

"Those rats must have been pretty strong to

break the bottles," D'Artagnan said to the man in an exaggerated manner.

"And my bacon! It, too, is gnawed!" cried the innkeeper.

"An enormous quantity of rats must live down there," D'Artagnan observed, barely able to hold in his laughter.

"You are right," Athos chuckled. "And the loss of his food and drink is just what this innkeeper deserves."

"Nevertheless, we will pay him," D'Artagnan said.

After they had paid the innkeeper and were riding back to Paris, D'Artagnan told Athos of his adventures. Porthos and Aramis listened attentively, though they had heard the story already.

"It was all the fault of Cardinal Richelieu and Milady," D'Artagnan concluded. "She is a beautiful woman, but extremely dangerous. It is no wonder she is marked with the *fleur-de-lis*."

"What!" Athos exclaimed with a look of shocked horror. "Please explain yourself."

D'Artagnan told of having accidentally seen the mark of the *fleur-de-lis* on Milady's shoulder.

"Then it must be she!" Athos said. "She was once the love of my life."

"What do you mean?" Aramis asked in surprise.

"The woman with the *fleur-de-lis*, the beautiful Milady—she was to be my wife. When we were engaged to be married, I did not know that in the past she had committed some serious crimes. On the day before our wedding was to take place, I chanced to see the brand on her shoulder. She fled from me, and I have never seen her since. I thought that perhaps she had gone to stay with the nuns so that she might repent, or that she had died."

"Do you love her still?" D'Artagnan asked. He understood for the first time why Athos often appeared to be lost in thought.

Athos smiled sadly. "I will love her always, but that will not change who she is. I am glad to learn that she is still alive, but it saddens me to hear that she uses her great beauty to evil ends."

"Perhaps we can stop her," D'Artagnan said.

"Yes, maybe we can," Athos agreed.

"All for one!" Aramis shouted.

"And one for all!" the others responded.

Chapter Eighteen

 Wishbone had heard the kids' voices, but he hadn't been able to stop for a chat. He had a job to do, even though hunting rats, like everything else, was a lot more fun when he shared the adventure with his friends. It wasn't his friends' fault that they couldn't keep up with him.

Mr. Brassfield, on the other hand, wasn't much fun to share adventure with at all.

Mr. Brassfield obviously doesn't understand my mission, either, Wishbone thought. *Imagine, trying to throw me out of the building—the very idea!*

Wishbone's nails clicked on the floor as he ran down the hallway. He looked this way and that for Mort. At the same time, he tried to avoid eviction by Mr. Brassfield, who had located him earlier in a classroom near the stairway.

When Wishbone came to the stairway, he had to make a sudden turn—either that, or run head first into the wall.

He chose the turn. His back legs slipped and slid on

the slick floor because it was hard for him to get any traction.

"Stealth Dog is out of control! Mayday! Mayday! Help!" he called.

Right when it seemed that Wishbone was going to crash into the wall, his back paws got a grip and he was able to make the turn, just avoiding Mr. Brassfield's outstretched hands.

"A pretty tight race, but Stealth Dog is still in the lead!" he said triumphantly.

Wishbone tore down the staircase, taking the steps two at a time. He gained a little ground on Mr. Brassfield.

Then two things happened at once: Wishbone heard voices at the foot of the staircase, and he saw something white and furry out of the corner of his eye.

"Helllooo! Mr. Brassfield, did you just see what I saw? It's a big, white—" Wishbone began.

"Stop right there, dog!" Mr. Brassfield yelled. "I've got you now!"

"—rat! Big rat! I've got you now, Mort!"

But Mort was still playing hard-to-get. He made another one-hundred-eighty-degree turn, sped around the corner of the staircase landing, then disappeared from sight.

Wishbone turned the corner right behind the rat. At the bottom of the staircase were David, Sam, and Joe.

"Joe! Sam! David! Mort's coming! Grab him!"

Mort skittered past the group before anyone even got a good look at him. But they did see Wishbone and Mr. Brassfield barreling down on them.

Wishbone ran between their legs. "Heads up, guys! Coming through!"

"Hey, Wishbone," Joe called. "What's going on, boy? What are you doing in here?"

"No dogs allowed in school," Mr. Brassfield said, but Wishbone didn't slow down.

"Dogs? There's no one here but us rat-catchers. Come on, guys, let's get Mort!" Wishbone said.

Wishbone could hear everyone joining the chase behind him.

I'm so happy that I've finally run into my three best friends. Now we're a team again, off to help one another in our common pursuit. It's just the same way that D'Artagnan must have felt when he and his three musketeer friends were finally reunited and returning together to Paris.

Chapter Nineteen

Unfortunately, D'Artagnan's troubles were not yet at an end, any more than Wishbone's were. Cardinal Richelieu and Milady continued to plot against him. Athos, Porthos, and Aramis agreed among themselves that they would help their friend find a way to defeat his enemies.

So one evening when D'Artagnan was at home, the three musketeers went to the cardinal's grand house.

There was a high wall around the gardens that surrounded the house, and the musketeers had a bit of difficulty climbing over it. Porthos assisted Aramis and Athos, but then he was stuck with no one to assist him in getting over the side of the wall. He was determined to make his way over the wall. As he climbed up, he made a great deal of noise.

Athos went to the wall and whispered, "Be quiet, Porthos. You sound like a herd of elephants!"

"If I had not helped you, you would still be outside the wall," Porthos said, panting. Finally, he managed to struggle to the top of the wall. "Get out of my way, or I will fall on you."

"Quiet!" Aramis warned. "Someone is coming."

Porthos dropped down to the ground as quietly as he could. Aramis led the way to where a group of statues stood deep in the shadows.

"We can hide here," Aramis said. "Perhaps we will hear something of interest."

Standing as silent as the statues that hid them, they heard Milady's voice.

"Let us go walk for a while in the garden, Cardinal Richelieu," she said. "It's lovely in the darkness."

The musketeers watched as Milady and the cardinal entered the garden. Their footsteps crunched on the gravel path. The sky was mostly cloudy, but the moon gave enough light so that the musketeers could see that Milady looked quite beautiful, as she always did. However, the conversation she was having with the cardinal was not a pretty one at all.

"Now that we are alone," she said to the cardinal, "tell me what you wished to speak to me about."

"I must ask you to undertake a very dangerous mission," the cardinal said.

Milady seemed excited at the prospect of danger. "Please, tell me what it is."

The cardinal looked at her and said, "I want you to assassinate the duke of Buckingham. He is an enemy of France, and somehow he foiled my plans with the diamonds. Now he must be removed."

"I will do it gladly," Milady said, without a hint of remorse. "But I must have something in return. I am not a mere cat's-paw to be used as you wish. I have my price."

The cardinal smiled. "Name it."

"You must give me the head of that wretched D'Artagnan."

The musketeers gasped upon hearing Milady's

request. Slight as the sound was, it caught the cardinal's ear, and he turned to look in their direction. They all froze in place, motionless, becoming a part of the statues by which they were concealed. Luckily, the cardinal was fooled. After a moment, he turned his attention back to Milady.

"But he is a courageous young fighter. He will not be easy to defeat," the cardinal said.

"That's why he's so dangerous," Milady replied. "And he fights for the wrong side. I believe that it was he as much as Buckingham who destroyed our plot to discredit the queen with the incident involving the diamond studs. I want him eliminated. I will trade you Buckingham's life for D'Artagnan's head. Otherwise, I will not help you."

The cardinal walked a few steps, deep in thought. Then he said, "Very well. I warned D'Artagnan that he could get hurt if he chose to serve the wrong master."

Aramis suddenly found himself overwhelmed with a desire to sneeze. He took a deep breath and was saved from betraying all of them by Porthos, who put a finger beneath his friend's nose.

"I am pleased that you see things my way," Milady told the cardinal. "Nevertheless, I would like to have something in writing, just in case there is any *confusion* later."

The cardinal hesitated for just a moment. Soon, however, he went to a bench, sat down, and wrote something on a piece of paper that had been inside a book he was carrying. He handed it to Milady just as the moon peeked out once more from behind the clouds, giving her enough light to read by.

She looked over the letter and said, "Thank you, Your Eminence. This *carte blanche* gives its holder immunity from prosecution for any wrongdoing. How comforting."

Wow! This is like the ultimate hall pass. It says that whoever is in possession of the *carte blanche* can do anything at any time, without any penalty.

"I must go now," the cardinal said. "Let me leave first. We must not be seen together."

As the cardinal left the garden, Milady smiled in triumph. While she stood there gloating, Porthos removed his finger from beneath Aramis's nose, and Aramis sneezed loudly.

Milady whirled around to see the musketeers. Aramis stepped away from the statues as the moon again emerged from behind the clouds.

"Sculpture is so lifelike these days," Aramis said. "Don't you agree, Milady?"

Milady turned to flee, but Porthos and Athos joined Aramis. The three encircled her and cut off her retreat. Milady looked from one to the other. "How dare you spy on me and His Eminence! You'll suffer for this! I'm not afraid of you!"

Athos took a step nearer to her, the moonlight falling on his face. "Hand over the *carte blanche*."

"You!" Milady spat. "I had hoped *never* to see you again."

"Yet here I am. Now, give me the letter."

"Never! It is my passport for revenge!"

"Come," Athos said as he drew nearer. "Be reasonable about this."

Milady put away the paper in a pocket of her dress. "If you want it, you must take it from me!"

The three musketeers moved toward her.

Milady whipped out a dagger from within the

folds of her dress and slashed at them. "Guards!" she screamed. "To the garden! The musketeers are here!"

Four of the cardinal's guards appeared out of the darkness, their swords drawn. Porthos and Aramis engaged them at once, taking on two swordsmen each. Their blades flashed in the moonlight.

Porthos forced his two opponents back into the rosebushes. The guards were soon hopping to avoid the thorns that clawed at their legs.

"Ha!" Porthos exclaimed, slashing at the men with his sword. "Did no one ever teach you not to walk in the flowers?"

One of his opponents got his legs tangled in the bushes and fell. Porthos soon injured one of the guards and then had only one man left to fight.

Aramis, meanwhile, was still occupied by the other two swordsmen, both of whom appeared to be his equal in fighting skills. "Porthos!" Aramis called. "A little help, please."

Porthos knew exactly what his friend needed. Taking a moment out from his own duel, he stuck the tip of his sword under the blade of the fallen guard and flipped the sword into the air. It arced through the moonlight, and Aramis snatched it from the air with his left hand.

"Now I have a sword for each of you," Aramis said to his adversaries. "And you will never defeat my two good arms."

He began parrying and thrusting with both blades, driving the surprised guards backward down the path. With a quick turn and a twirl of his cape, he forced them against a low bench, which struck the backs of their legs. They both fell, and Aramis instantly had his sword points at their throats.

"Yield or die!" Aramis said.

While all this was going on, Athos confronted the woman whom at one time he had loved and had almost married—the woman who had once broken his heart. He refused to draw his sword against her, though she continued to slash at him with her dagger. He dodged to the left and then to the right, waiting for his chance to grab her arm.

"I hate you!" she exclaimed.

Athos looked at her and thought about her terrible crimes. Then his mind drifted for a moment to the happier times he had spent with Milady. She took advantage of his loss of concentration to make a wicked slice with her dagger. The sharp blade razored through Athos's jacket and cut a thin red line down his side.

Milady expected Athos to leap backward. Instead, he jumped toward her, grabbing her wrist and bending back her arm.

"Drop the dagger," he said sharply. "And give the letter to me at once."

"Never! You will have to kill me first."

"Perhaps not," Porthos said, stepping up to her. He had taken care of the second guard with a well-placed blow. Now he had come to assist his friend. While Athos held Milady's arm tightly, Porthos took the dagger from her hand.

Milady hissed at him and tried to claw his face with her free hand.

Porthos dodged her sharp nails and took hold of her arm. "Don't be catty," he said. "It's very unbecoming behavior."

Athos bent Milady's wrist a bit more. "Take the paper, Porthos."

Porthos removed the letter from Milady's pocket and handed it to Athos, who tucked it inside his shirt.

"Where is Aramis?" Athos asked.

"Here," Aramis called. He walked over to them with the two guards in front of him. He held the point of a sword at each man's back.

Athos bent down and plucked a flower from the garden. "Here," he said, giving it to Milady. "A symbol of my former esteem."

Milady hissed at him, and her face was twisted with rage.

"Someday," Athos said, "the executioner will claim you. If he does not, I must."

"I'll see you dead before that day ever comes!" Milady snapped.

"Be that as it may," Porthos said, "I believe that we should be going. We have overstayed our welcome here."

"I agree," Athos said. He turned to the two guards who remained standing. "Escort Milady inside, and do not bother raising a cry. We will be gone before you can return."

Porthos shoved Milady toward the guards. They accompanied Milady inside. Athos watched them for a moment with a heavy heart, until Aramis touched him on the shoulder.

"We must go, my friend," he said.

"You are right," Athos replied.

He shook his had sadly, and the three friends walked away.

"I suggest that we use the gate this time," Porthos said. "It's much quicker, and we're not trying to hide."

"Very well," Aramis said.

The next day, the musketeers met D'Artagnan at the barracks where the king's guards trained. They told their friend about Milady's plot against his life and handed him the *carte blanche*.

"I'm afraid that Milady was a bit upset with us for taking the letter," Athos told D'Artagnan. "She has already asked for your head. She may report you as a traitor and hope to arrange your death that way."

D'Artagnan waved the letter. "If she does, she'll find that I have an ace up my sleeve. Thank you, my friends, but I like my head just where it is."

"We were happy to be able to be of help to you," Porthos said.

Aramis pointed across the courtyard of the Hôtel de Tréville. "Watch out, my friends! The cardinal's men are approaching."

The guards marched up to D'Artagnan. Their leader said, "D'Artagnan, I seek you in the name of the cardinal. You are under arrest."

"*Moi*? Surely you jest," D'Artagnan said.

"Surrender your sword to me, *monsieur*," the guard continued. "I am ordered to present you to His Eminence, Cardinal Richelieu."

Athos drew his sword, as did his companions. He put the tip of the blade right on the guard's neck. "How convenient. We happen to be going in that direction ourselves. We would be glad to take D'Artagnan to His Eminence. Upon our word, D'Artagnan will not leave us. We will see that he reaches his destination."

"Very well," the guard said. "Upon your words. He is your responsibility now."

The guard signaled to his men, and they withdrew. The musketeers sheathed their swords.

So now I'm the cardinal's prisoner, D'Artagnan thought. *It looks as if I might need that* carte blanche *letter sooner than I thought!*

Chapter Twenty

Soon enough, D'Artagnan found himself once again sitting on his haunches in the velvet-covered chair on the other side of the massive desk across from Cardinal Richelieu. There was more light in the room this time because the cardinal had pulled open the heavy curtains. He stood with his back to the desk, looking out the window where the branches of a tall oak tree swayed slowly in the morning breeze.

I wonder what he sees out there, D'Artagnan thought. *Maybe there's a cat in that tree.*

After a few minutes, the cardinal turned to glare at D'Artagnan. "So, D'Artagnan, you chose to ignore my warnings. Now you see the result. Serious charges have been brought against you. You will probably lose your head because of them."

"I see," D'Artagnan replied calmly.

"You do not seem upset. Do you realize that I am both judge and jury?"

"Exactly. And as judge and jury, you have already written my pardon. Please take a look at this, Cardinal Richelieu."

D'Artagnan set a paw on the *carte blanche*. He had placed it on the desk while the cardinal was gazing out the window.

The cardinal picked up the paper and stared at it for a moment. Then he began to read it aloud. "'It is by my order, and for the good of the state, that the bearer of this letter has done what he has done.'"

As the realization that he held the *carte blanche* dawned on him, the cardinal looked dazed. He crumpled up the letter, slapped it down on his desk, and sat down heavily in his high-backed chair.

"I'll give you three guesses as to whose handwriting that is. You won't need the last two," D'Artagnan said.

The cardinal was visibly annoyed. "I believe that the handwriting is mine."

"Hey! You're nearly as good a guesser as I am!" said D'Artagnan.

"But *I* have the letter now," the cardinal said. "And *you* don't. . . . Guards!"

Two men rushed into the room, their hands at their sword hilts.

"This man attacked me! Remove him at once to the prison."

"Oh, no, Your Eminence," D'Artagnan said. "It won't be so easy as that!"

The two men separated from each other and charged toward D'Artagnan, one on either side of the long table that ran down the middle of the room. D'Artagnan drew his sword and jumped atop the table. He lashed out with his blade to the right and to the left, fending off the blows of the guards.

Tiring of that game, one of the guards jumped onto the table with him. D'Artagnan took his sword in his mouth and leaped up onto a chandelier, swinging it toward his foe. The guard tried to duck out of his way, but the rim of the chandelier struck him just under the chin. He tumbled backward and fell across the cardinal's desk. The cardinal quickly scrambled out of the way.

On the next swing of the chandelier, D'Artagnan stuck the tip of his sword into the letter, flipped it into the air, and caught it. Then, as he swung back, he hacked at the blade of the remaining guard's sword. He struck it with such a solid blow that the sword broke in half. D'Artagnan jumped down from the chandelier onto the guard, putting all four paws on the man's chest.

"Do you yield?" D'Artagnan asked.

"I do," the guard said.

"Very well, then," D'Artagnan replied. He got off the guard's chest and faced the cardinal. "And you, Your Eminence, do you admit that you wrote this letter and that it is mine by right?"

After a few moments had passed in silence, the cardinal said, "I do."

"Then I am free to go?"

"Yes . . . but wait a moment."

The cardinal took a quill pen from his desk and scratched out some words on another piece of paper. Then he handed the new paper to D'Artagnan.

"Now," the cardinal said, "give me the *carte blanche,* and I will give you something better. This is a commission to be a lieutenant in the musketeers. The place for the name is blank. You might wish to write it in yourself."

I have three friends who deserve this more than I do. But I'll take it! thought D'Artagnan.

"You are a brave youth, D'Artagnan. Do with the commission what you will," the cardinal said.

With those words, Cardinal Richelieu handed the paper to D'Artagnan.

D'Artagnan raced all the way back to the courtyard of the Hôtel de Tréville with the commission paper in his mouth. His three close friends were seated on a bench beside a table. D'Artagnan jumped up on the bench next to them. Wagging his tail, he dropped the commission paper to the tabletop.

The musketeers read it eagerly. When they had finished, D'Artagnan said, "One of you should take this. All of you are more deserving of this honor than I am."

Aramis smiled. "Oh, no, my friend. No one is more worthy than you. You have proved that to all of us, time and again."

"True," Porthos said. "On the other hand, it is also true that I taught D'Artagnan all that he knows."

Athos drew his sword and smiled. "Is that so? Then you may wish to prove it to me. *En garde!*"

Aramis drew his sword as well to join the fun.

Porthos sighed. "I suppose that I will have to teach both of you a lesson."

He drew out his sword and assumed the proper fencing stance.

D'Artagnan watched the clowning of the three musketeers with affection. It seemed to him that no one, anywhere, could have finer, braver, or more noble companions.

With that thought, he put his paw print onto the blank space on the commission paper.

A musketeer! I hardly thought it possible. And a lieutenant, as well! This is a dream come true! En garde!

Hopping down from the bench, D'Artagnan drew his sword and joined his friends. Together, the *four* musketeers cheered lustily.

"All for one, and one for all!"

Chapter Twenty-One

*W*ishbone had the rat trapped at the bottom of a shelf.

"All right, I've got him cornered now! Okay, Mr. Brassfield, time for you to take over!" Wishbone said.

Wishbone hopped up on a chair just as Mr. Brassfield entered the room. Mort, seeing his chance to escape, darted out from under the table, right at Mr. Brassfield's feet.

"That's it! Get him! Come on, Mr. Brassfield! Are you a man, or a mouse? Grab that rat!" Wishbone said.

Instead of grabbing Mort, Mr. Brassfield gave a yell and jumped up on a computer table.

"A little help here, Mr. Brassfield. We need to work together on this if we're going to catch that rat," Wishbone explained.

"Wow! He's gotten big!" Mr. Brassfield said.

"Uh-huh. Well, that just goes to show you—never send a man to do a dog's job. Stand back, Mr. Brassfield, and watch a real rat-catcher at work," Wishbone said, as he jumped from the chair to a lab table, where he sat, scanning the room. "All right, what now? A plan—that's what I need. A quick plan," Wishbone said.

Mort scurried across the floor, passing right under the table where Wishbone stood. There was a cracker crumb on the floor, dropped by some careless student. As Wishbone watched the scene, Mort stopped to examine the crumb. Mort sniffed it, then picked it up in his paws and began to nibble it.

"Your appetite has gotten the better of you, rat, and you're going to regret it—just as soon as I come up with that plan. . . . Aha! Is that a box I see?" Wishbone said.

It was indeed a box, and Wishbone began to nose it quietly toward the edge of the table.

"Stealth Dog to bombardier. Come in, bombardier. We have the target in sight," Wishbone said.

Wishbone left the box and took a quick peek over the edge of the table.

"I've got the altitude, bombardier," Wishbone said.

Wishbone concentrated on his target.

"Ready . . ." he continued.

Wishbone pushed the box right to the edge of the table. He took another glance down at Mort, who was still nibbling away at the cracker crumb.

"Aim . . ."

Wishbone gauged the distance carefully and then got back behind the box.

"Bombs away!" Wishbone cried.

Wishbone nudged the box over the table's edge. It fell straight down, trapping Mort underneath.

"Got you that time, Mort! Yes! Stealth Dog strikes again!" Wishbone said triumphantly.

Wishbone settled back on his haunches, pleased

with himself and his good work. Mr. Brassfield walked gingerly over to the box, just as Joe, Sam, and David entered the room.

Wishbone sat down on the table and looked down at the box.

"Well, guys, what do you think?"

"I'm sorry about all this confusion, Mr. Brassfield," Joe said. "I don't have any idea how Wishbone got in here."

"You don't have to apologize, Joe," Mr. Brassfield said. "Wishbone caught Mort. He's trapped him under this box."

"Thank you, citizen," Wishbone said. "All in a day's work for Stealth Dog."

Mr. Brassfield bent over and tapped the box with a finger.

"Good boy, Wishbone," Joe said.

"As far as I'm concerned," Mr. Brassfield said, "Wishbone can come to school any time he wants to. He can be my guest."

"Good idea. I'd like to have a little guided tour of the building right now. Could we start with the lunch room?" Wishbone asked.

Still bending down, Mr. Brassfield reached for the box. Wishbone hopped down off the table, using Mr. Brassfield's back as a stepping-stone. Startled, Mr. Brassfield tried to stand up, but he lost his balance and stumbled forward into the skeleton, and the plastic bones clicked against one another.

"Oops!" Wishbone said.

Mr. Brassfield tried to keep from falling by grabbing the skeleton. He struggled with the skeleton, and its arms and legs bounced as Mr. Brassfield became more and more entangled with it.

"What a lovely couple you two make! May I have the next dance?" Wishbone asked.

Mr. Brassfield couldn't keep his feet under him. He fell to the floor, and the skeleton landed on top of him. Joe, Sam, and David tried not to laugh.

"I've changed my mind!" Mr. Brassfield yelled, tossing the skeleton aside. "No dogs allowed in school!"

He jumped up and started toward Wishbone, who ran out the doorway.

"Here we go again!" Wishbone exclaimed.

"Come back here, you dog!" Mr. Brassfield yelled, leaving the room at a quick pace. "Stop!"

"I think we'd better follow them," Wishbone heard Joe say.

"We've got to go help," David said.

"Right," Sam said. "Wishbone's a hero."

Wishbone could hear running sounds, and he knew his friends were right behind Mr. Brassfield.

Even halfway down the hall, Wishbone could

hear the scratching of a box scraping on a floor. He could picture the box moving along the floor—looking as if it was moving on its own. Wishbone knew that Mort was on the move again. Once Wishbone lost Mr. Brassfield, he knew that Stealth Dog would be going back on duty!

About Alexandre Dumas

*L*ike D'Artagnan, the young hero of *The Three Musketeers*, Alexandre Dumas arrived in Paris with little more than a recommendation to a friend of his father's. Born in 1802, the grandson of a Haitian slave, Dumas became one of France's most popular writers.

Best known for his action-packed adventure stories like *The Three Musketeers*, *The Man in the Iron Mask*, and *The Count of Monte Cristo*, Dumas is also famous for penning enough novels, articles, and dramas to fill 300 volumes. More than 200 movies have been based on them!

A writer of tremendous talent and energy, Dumas liked to do everything on a grand scale—once he invited 600 guests to a party at his magnificent Château de Monte Cristo! Living life fully, in the spirit of the characters he created, Dumas loved adventure and romance. In his lifetime he fought a number of duels and participated in three revolutions. His son, also named Alexandre Dumas, inherited his father's literary talent and became a famous author in his own right.

About *The Three Musketeers*

*W*ritten more than one hundred and fifty years ago, *The Three Musketeers* remains one of the most famous and well-loved historical adventures. The story is full of swashbuckling action, comedy, and romance. Alexandre Dumas's novel of political rivalry and intrigue in seventeenth-century France

inspired two sequels and made the names of four unforgettable friends—D'Artagnan, Porthos, Athos, and Aramis—familiar to millions of readers around the world.

Hot-headed, big-hearted, and happy to risk their lives at one another's side, the musketeers are the best of blades and the best of friends in France. Their camaraderie, forged in the heat of battle, defies all odds (and a few assassination attempts) and remains firm to the end. To this day the musketeers' rousing cry of "All for one, and one for all!" stands for undying friendship and loyalty.

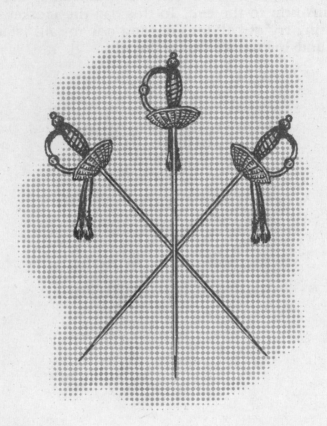

About Bill Crider

*U*nlike D'Artagnan and the musketeers, Bill Crider has never been in an actual sword fight. However, he did take fencing lessons in college and learned any number of clever thrusts and parries.

Bill teaches English at Alvin Community College, in Alvin, Texas. Besides writing *Muttketeer!*, he is the author of more than thirty novels, many of them westerns and mysteries written for adults. For young readers, his series about Mike Gonzo includes *Mike Gonzo and the Sewer Monster*, *Mike Gonzo and the Almost Invisible Man*, and *Mike Gonzo and the UFO Terror*. He is also the author of *A Vampire Named Fred*.

Bill is a collector of vintage baseball cards, old books, and toy alligators. He is particularly proud of his complete set of 1953 Topps cards. His ever-growing collection of alligators has now taken over much of his house, to the amazement of his wife, Judy, and their four cats—Speedo, Jeoffry, Sam, and Gerri.

Now Playing on Your VCR...

Two exciting **WISHBONE®** stories on video!

Ready for an adventure? Then leap right in with **Wishbone**™ as he takes you on a thrilling journey through two great action-packed stories. First, there are haunted houses, buried treasure, and mysterious graves in two back-to-back episodes of *A Tail in Twain*, starring **Wishbone** as Tom Sawyer. Then, no one is more powerful than **Wishbone**, in *Hercules Unleashed*, featuring exciting new footage! It's more fun than a flea dip! It's **Wishbone** on home video.

WISHBONE™

Available wherever videos are sold.